MY COUSIN RACHEL

A PLAY
BY DIANA MORGAN

FROM THE NOVEL
BY DAPHNE DU MAURIER

DRAMATISTS
PLAY SERVICE
INC.

MY COUSIN RACHEL
Copyright © 1980, Du Maurier Productions, Ltd. and Diana Morgan
Based on Daphne Du Maurier's Novel "My Cousin Rachel"
Copyright © 1951, Daphne Du Maurier

All Rights Reserved

SPECIAL NOTE

CAST

SEECOMBE

JAMES

PHILIP ASHLEY

LOUISE KENDALL

NICHOLAS KENDALL

RACHEL ASHLEY

ANTONIO RAINALDI

The action takes place at Barton Hall in Cornwall.

TIME: Sometime in the last century.

NOTE: The curtain will not be dropped between the scenes. Lapses of time will be denoted by the fading down and fading up of lights.

MY COUSIN RACHEL

ACT ONE

SCENE 1

The Curtain Rises on The Hall at Barton:
*This is the Great Hall of a large Cornish Manor House. A big
window* U.C. *and a door leading to the drive and the garden. A
staircase* R. *leading to a gallery.* D.L. *a door leading to the
servants' quarters.* D.R. *a door leading to the dining room.
It is dark. Candles flicker.
A distant rumble of thunder.
Seecombe, the elderly, shabby steward enters, carrying a candle
in a jam pot. He is followed by James pulling on a jerkin.
Seecombe waves the boy out to the front door and puts down the
jam pot. A horse is heard neighing. James re-enters carrying a
valise.*

JAMES. Do I put it in Master Philip's room?
SEECOMBE. No, put it in Mr. Ashley's old room. (*As James goes to
the stairs, half-followed by Seecombe, Philip Ashley enters. He is young,
sensitive looking, obviously very exhausted. He wears a coat with a cape
and carries a small travelling case. Seecombe takes the case and hands it to
James.*) See that the fire's still going. Go on, lad! (*James goes
upstairs.*)
PHILIP. I beg that no-one makes a fuss, Seecombe.
SEECOMBE. We've all been so worried, Mr. Philip. It's been such
a time. And we were afraid you might take the fever like poor Mr.
Ashley.
PHILIP. I'm not ill, Seecombe. Only very tired. It's a long journey
from Florence.
SEECOMBE. Best part of three weeks.
PHILIP. Yes. Well, I'm for bed. We'll talk in the morning.
SEECOMBE. I took the liberty of informing Mr. Kendall of your
return, sir. I sent James over to Pelyn when I got your letter.
PHILIP. Thank you.

SEECOMBE. And I also took the liberty of making up the bed in poor Mr. Ashley's room.

PHILIP. Ambrose's room. (*Pause.*) Yes, that will do very well. (*James comes downstairs.*)

SEECOMBE. You must be hungry, sir. I'll send up a tray.

PHILIP. No nothing to eat—just a hot brandy and lemon. Goodnight. (*Seecombe gives him the candle and he goes slowly upstairs, opens the door and when he shuts it the stage is in darkness. There is a distant rumble of thunder and the wind rises.*)

FADE DOWN LIGHTS

FADE UP

ACT ONE

SCENE 2

The next morning.
Sunshine streaming through the great window reveals the shabby interior—dust and cobwebs everywhere. The door bell clangs. Silence. It clangs again. Seecombe enters and crosses towards the door and pulls it open. Louise Kendall enters. She is a pretty girl of about eighteen, hoydenish, wearing a riding habit. She is followed by Nicholas Kendall her father, an attractive man in his fifties. He wears a black arm-band and carries a leather case.

LOUISE. (*Radiantly.*) Seecombe, where is he?

SEECOMBE. Mr. Philip came late and went straight to his bed, Miss Louise. He was worn out. Foreign parts is a long way off as I said—and they don't come no foreigner than Italy—on account of the Italians no doubt . . . I'll tell him you're here, Miss.

LOUISE. Hurry, Seecombe, hurry . . . !

KENDALL. Don't be so impatient, Louise. (*Seecombe goes off upstairs and disappears.*)

LOUISE. (*Removing her gloves.*) I hope he won't be long—I'm dying to hear . . .

KENDALL. Louise—!

LOUISE. Father?

KENDALL. You're a sensible girl, Louise. I beg you to be so now . . .

6

LOUISE. Oh, father—!

KENDALL. Be careful what you say to Philip. Ambrose Ashley was everything to Philip—the only family he has ever known. He was much more than a cousin to him—he was Father, Mother, brother, friend. Ambrose's death is a sad thing for all of us—but it is a tragedy for Philip. He may want to talk about it—on the other hand he may not. I beg that you do not rush him. He'll need time to find himself, to put the past eighteen months behind him and realise that he is now master of Barton. (*Seecombe comes downstairs.*)

SEECOMBE. Mr. Philip will be with you presently.

KENDALL. Thank you.

SEECOMBE. Some refreshment, sir?

KENDALL. Not at the moment Seecombe.

SEECOMBE. Miss Louise? (*Louise shakes her head. Seecombe exits.*)

LOUISE. How strange it is. Ambrose dead and Philip . . . How strange everything is—Ambrose marrying like that was strange.

KENDALL. Yes.

LOUISE. Meeting this Cousin Rachel in Florence and marrying her after a few weeks. Oh, I do wonder what she's like!

KENDALL. Now, Louise!

LOUISE. I expect she's very fascinating.

KENDALL. Why?

LOUISE. Well she caught an old bachelor like Ambrose—she must be fascinating.

KENDALL. Ambrose wasn't old. My age.

LOUISE. Well you're hardly a chicken, Father. Never mind, Mary Pascoe said you must have been very fascinating—once. (*Kendall snorts. Philip runs down the staircase and greets them.*)

PHILIP. Louise. Uncle Nick.

KENDALL. Good to see you, Philip. What sort of a journey did you have?

PHILIP. It was very rough in the Bay. Louise, I brought you this. (*He hands her a small package.*)

LOUISE. (*Delighted.*) Oh Phil! (*She starts to open it.*)

KENDALL. You spoil her.

PHILIP. So do you. By the way did Seecombe offer you any refreshment?

KENDALL. Yes. But we dined early thank you.

LOUISE. (*Displaying necklace.*) Oh Phil—it's beautiful! How clever of you. I love amber. Did you know?

PHILIP. As a matter of fact I asked the man in the shop what a young lady would like. I'm not very good at that sort of thing.

7

LOUISE. (*Disappointed.*) I see. (*Short pause.*)

PHILIP. Well Uncle Nick, you'll be wanting to hear my news.

KENDALL. Yes.

PHILIP. It's difficult to know where to begin.

KENDALL. You arrived in Florence . . . ?

PHILIP. Yes, and went straight to the villa. When I got there the butler told me that Ambrose had been dead for three weeks.

LOUISE. It must have been a dreadful shock. Poor Philip.

PHILIP. Yes.

KENDALL. What then?

PHILIP. I asked for Mrs. Ashley.

KENDALL. Yes?

PHILIP. I was told that she had left Florence immediately after the funeral, taking all Ambrose's possessions with her.

LOUISE. So you didn't see her?

PHILIP. No.

LOUISE. Oh, I *am* disappointed. Ever since Ambrose wrote and said he'd married his Cousin Rachel, I've longed to know what she was like. I was just saying to Father that I was sure she must be very fascinating or Ambrose would never have married her, wasn't I, Father?

KENDALL. Stop chattering, Louise. Go on Philip.

PHILIP. I went to see her man of business, Signor Rainaldi. Ambrose had mentioned him in his letters. I didn't like him. In fact I detested him.

KENDALL. What was wrong with him?

PHILIP. I can rely on you, Uncle Nick and you, Louise, can't I?

KENDALL. I've been your guardian for 24 years, Philip.

PHILIP. Did you wonder why I rushed out to Italy so suddenly?

KENDALL. Ambrose was ill. (*Philip takes a letter from his pocket and hands it to Kendall.*)

PHILIP. Read that. (*Kendall begins to read it.*) Aloud. I want Louise to hear.

KENDALL. (*Reading.*) ". . . There is no one I can trust. She watches me continually. Sometimes I think that money is the only way to her heart. I don't trust Rainaldi, nor the doctor he recommended to me. I shall try to smuggle this letter out of the house. I will beat them yet . . . why must she lie to me all the time? . . . Ambrose." Poor Ambrose. Poor fellow. Just like his father.

PHILIP. What do you mean?

KENDALL. His father died of brain fever, too. In his last days he turned against everyone he loved, particularly his wife.

8

PHILIP. Ambrose's marriage was a great shock.

KENDALL. I know. But given time it might have proved a blessing.

PHILIP. A blessing?

KENDALL. Yes. This house needed a woman. The monastic life you lived here was unnatural.

PHILIP. We were happy.

KENDALL. You thought you were happy. Go on.

PHILIP. Then Ambrose gets ill and I get that letter. I go to Italy, find he has died very suddenly, find that his wife has disappeared, get no satisfaction out of this Rainaldi fellow, come back yesterday to find a last letter from Ambrose has arrived during my absence. (*He takes out another letter.*) It's very short . . . I'll read it to you. "Come quickly . . . she has done for me . . . Rachel, my torment . . ."

KENDALL. Well?

PHILIP. Don't you understand? Don't you see what I am implying?

KENDALL. Certainly. You are implying that there is something—something not . . . damn it all, Philip, you are implying that Mrs. Ashley had something to do with her husband's death.

PHILIP. Yes.

KENDALL. You'd better be careful, my boy. If you spread a rumour like this—and it got to her ears . . .

PHILIP. I wish it to get to her ears.

LOUISE. Philip!

KENDALL. You're talking like a madman, Philip. Now, you listen to me. Ambrose who had not been well, gets a bad attack of Roman fever. It goes to his brain exactly as it did to his father's. He died in Rome when Ambrose was still a child. You have no evidence, no evidence whatever against Mrs. Ashley. She had nothing to gain from her husband's death—and everything to lose. I am amazed that we have not heard of any new Will drawn up in her favour. As things stand you get everything and she gets nothing. So you be careful, Philip.

PHILIP. Just wait until I find out where she is—that's all.

KENDALL. *I* can tell you where she is.

PHILIP. *You* can?

KENDALL. She's in Plymouth. I had a letter from her this morning—she has brought all Ambrose's possessions with her. I am going to ask her to stay with Louise and me while she is in England. She is the window of my oldest friend.

LOUISE. Oh, Father! How fascinating . . .

PHILIP. In Plymouth . . .

KENDALL. She has also brought with her a great number of plants and seeds which she and Ambrose had collected. It was their love of gardening that first brought them together.

PHILIP. (*Slowly.*) The villa had a beautiful garden.

LOUISE. Then I shall see her at last! Oh—I do wonder what she's like.

KENDALL. I shall write to her tonight conveying the invitation.

PHILIP. No. She is Ambrose's widow. She must come here.

KENDALL. After what you've just been saying?

PHILIP. It would look very strange if she stayed elsewhere.

KENDALL. Agreed. But if you are going to accuse her . . .

PHILIP. (*Interrupting.*) I am not going to accuse her.

KENDALL. A few moments ago . . .

PHILIP. (*Interrupting.*) Tell her that Philip Ashley is a plain man and that Barton is a plain man's home—but that she is welcome.

KENDALL. Can I trust you, Philip to behave properly towards the poor woman?

PHILIP. I give you my word, Uncle Nick.

KENDALL. Very well. Now I must go and see old Tamblyn. There's been some trouble with his lease. Louise?

LOUISE. I think I'll stay for a bit, Father. Perhaps Philip will see me home.

PHILIP. Of course. (*Kendall makes for the main door. He pauses there.*)

KENDALL. Philip . . .

PHILIP. It's all right, Uncle Nick. (*Kendall goes out.*)

LOUISE. Oh, Phil—isn't it fascinating? We shall see her at last. I'm so excited. What do you think she looks like?

PHILIP. Like a snake.

LOUISE. I don't. I see her tall and stately—a real Roman matron. How old is she?

PHILIP. I've no idea. She has rheumatism—I know that—that's why she and Ambrose didn't come back last Winter.

LOUISE. Oh, then she must be quite old. Well on in her thirties. Little and bent and going gray . . . Phil . . .

PHILIP. Yes.

LOUISE. Do you—do you really think there was something—well, odd about Ambrose's death?

PHILIP. Yes.

10

LOUISE. But what can you do about it?

PHILIP. I can watch her. I shall know.

LOUISE. If she is—what you think—won't you be a bit frightened?

PHILIP. Frightened? Of a woman?

LOUISE. You don't know any women.

PHILIP. I know you.

LOUISE. I'm only a girl.

PHILIP. I am not in the least frightened of my cousin Rachel. She should be frightened of *me*. (*Louise bursts out laughing.*)

LOUISE. Philip, really!

PHILIP. I mean it.

LOUISE. Of all the pompous . . .

PHILIP. I mean it. (*Louise stops laughing abruptly.*)

LOUISE. How peculiar . . .

PHILIP. What is?

LOUISE. To see you looking like that. Like a stranger.

PHILIP. Rubbish.

LOUISE. Do you remember that old gypsy we met at Penhallow Fair?

PHILIP. Vaguely. Why?

LOUISE. She said you were like a sunlit pool—but only on the surface.

PHILIP. What *are* you talking about?

LOUISE. I've known you all my life.

PHILIP. What of it?

LOUISE. For a moment you were a stranger. I think I'd better be going.

PHILIP. As you wish. (*There is a pause as Louise picks up her riding crop.*)

LOUISE. I suppose you'll be going in to Plymouth to meet Mrs. Ashley.

PHILIP. No.

LOUISE. But, Philip . . .

PHILIP. I shall send the carriage.

LOUISE. But, Philip, you must go.

PHILIP. Why?

LOUISE. She is your guest—Ambrose's widow.

PHILIP. I am far too busy to waste time going to Plymouth. I shall leave instructions with the servants.

LOUISE. But it's such bad manners.

PHILIP. Don't try to teach me how to behave, Louise.

LOUISE. Why not? Someone should teach you common courtesy.

PHILIP. Someone should teach you to mind your own business. (*They stand glaring at each other. Louise breaks away and runs out. Seecombe enters.*) Seecombe, Mrs. Ashley is in England and will be coming to stay here.

SEECOMBE. (*Open mouthed.*) Mr. Ambrose's wife?

PHILIP. Mr. Ashley's widow.

SEECOMBE. Coming here?

PHILIP. Yes. You'd better get the pink room ready.

SEECOMBE. The floor boards have gone, sir.

PHILIP. The room over the library then.

SEECOMBE. It's got the woodworm.

PHILIP. Lady Mary's Chamber.

SEECOMBE. She walks most nights.

PHILIP. Damn it, Seecombe, what's wrong with the Oak Room?

SEECOMBE. Mice, Mr. Philip.

PHILIP. Get out Seecombe and if a room isn't ready by tomorrow afternoon I'll—I'll have you beaten with rods.

SEECOMBE. Very good, sir. Will that be all, sir?

PHILIP. More than enough! (*Roars.*) Out, Out! (*Seecombe goes. Philip shakes himself as if trying to clear his head from bewilderment.*) Tomorrow . . . coming tomorrow . . .

FADE OUT

FADE UP

ACT ONE

SCENE 3

A few days later. Evening.
Seecombe, is arranging flowers in silver rose-bowl. Philip enters by the main door.

PHILIP. What on earth are you doing, Seecombe?

SEECOMBE. Ladies like flowers in a room, Mr. Philip.

PHILIP. She's come?

SEECOMBE. Madam arrived at four o'clock. She said she would

12

dine in her room. James took her up a tray. At what hour will you dine, sir?

PHILIP. I dined in Bodmin. That will be all, Seecombe.

SEECOMBE. Very good, Mr. Philip. Madam asked to be informed when you arrived.

PHILIP. Well, inform her then. (*Seecombe inclines his head, goes up the stairs and knocks at a door.*)

SEECOMBE. Mr. Philip has returned, madam.

RACHEL. (*Offstage.*) Thank you, Seecombe. (*Seecombe comes down the stairs and exits through the servant's door. Philip moves restlessly about, clenching and unclenching his hands. The door upstairs opens and Rachel emerges, carrying a candle which illuminates her face. She comes slowly downstairs. At the foot of the stairs, she pauses and looks across at Philip.*) Ambrose . . . you are so like . . . (*She is a beautiful woman in her early thirties, tall and slender. She is dressed exquisitely in black. Philip moves forward.*)

PHILIP. Welcome to Barton, Cousin Rachel.

RACHEL. Thank you.

PHILIP. I regret I was not at home to welcome you.

RACHEL. You are a busy man. Ambrose told me how hard you worked. I quite understand.

PHILIP. I hope the servants have made you quite comfortable.

RACHEL. Very comfortable, thank you. (*Pause. She sits down.*) You must be wondering why I came to England. It was on your account—and Ambrose's.

PHILIP. Indeed?

RACHEL. He thought the world of you. "My Philip"—he would say. I know he would like you to have his personal possessions and he would have wanted the plants and shrubs we had so lovingly collected to find their proper home.

PHILIP. He loved the garden.

RACHEL. He loved everything about Barton. He used to talk about it by the hour. Bore Town and Borden's Meadow, Kemp Close and Beef Park, Kilmore and Beacon Field, the Twenty Acres and the West Hills.

PHILIP. (*Surprised.*) You seem to know the names of all the Barton lands.

RACHEL. He was so looking forward to showing them to me. We would sit in the courtyard at the villa, drinking our tisane, and instead of the sunshine I would see the grey seas breaking over Star Point and hear the seagulls crying.

PHILIP. This is your first visit to England?

RACHEL. Yes. My first husband, Count Sangaletti used to promise to bring me here for a visit but he was killed in an accident. From what I have seen of the countryside, Cornwell is very lovely. Very wild and exciting.

PHILIP. (*Abruptly.*) You know I came to Florence?

RACHEL. Yes. Signor Rainaldi wrote and told me. It must have been terrible for you. I wish I had known you were coming.

PHILIP. Ambrose wrote and begged me.

RACHEL. I know he was very anxious to see you.

PHILIP. Did he know how ill he was?

RACHEL. Possibly. But he was homesick—and you represented home to him.

PHILIP. He died very suddenly.

RACHEL. He had seemed better, less . . . less strange.

PHILIP. Strange?

RACHEL. When he first became ill, nothing I, or the doctors, could do would satisfy him. It was as if we had become his enemies.

PHILIP. Indeed?

RACHEL. It is often so. Pressure on the brain, the doctors told me. Then he suddenly seemed better—more like the Ambrose I knew and loved. We began to make plans. And then one evening . . .

PHILIP. Yes?

RACHEL. I was sitting by his bed. He seemed asleep. Then he . . . he opened his eyes and said: "Rachel" and fell back on the pillows . . . we had only been married eighteen months. (*There is a pause.*)

PHILIP. (*Awkwardly.*) May I get you a glass of wine?

RACHEL. Thank you no. Presently Seecombe will bring me some hot water and I will make the tisane that Ambrose and I loved. I asked him—oh, I do hope you don't mind.

PHILIP. Of course not. (*Pause.*)

RACHEL. How lovely this house is.

PHILIP. It's pretty shabby. Ambrose and I always intended doing something about it, but we never did. (*Pause.*)

RACHEL. I have a confession to make.

PHILIP. Oh?

RACHEL. I have been so jealous of you.

PHILIP. Jealous . . . ?

14

RACHEL. Your name was always on Ambrose's lip's. He told me that when your parents died he brought you up. You were so close. I had such pictures of you. Spoilt, I thought. Priggish, I thought. Did you wonder about me?

PHILIP. Yes.

RACHEL. And pictured me as a scheming Italian widow. (*Philip looks extremely uncomfortable. Rachel bursts out laughing.*) Philip, I may be Italian, and a widow, but I am far from scheming. How else did you picture me?

PHILIP. Older. Not so . . .

RACHEL. Not so what?

PHILIP. Not so—easy to talk to.

RACHEL. Thank you. We should talk easily together, you and I. We have so much in common—Ambrose, Barton, the house and the garden. When will you show me round the estate?

PHILIP. On Monday . can you ride?

RACHEL. Not well.

PHILIP. We have a steady horse called Dolabella, who would suit you.

RACHEL. What a charming name—Dolabella.

PHILIP. It was Ambrose's name for her.

RACHEL. Cyprian, Angus, Thunderer, Spick and Span . . .

PHILIP. You know all the horses.

RACHEL. And the dogs, Brimstone, Treacle, Flare, Sammy, Joshua. Why do you look at me like that?

PHILIP. Funny . . . we've only just met but I feel as if I'd known you a long a time.

RACHEL. Tell me, Philip, were you, perhaps, just a little bit jealous of me, too? (*Pause.*)

PHILIP. Yes.

RACHEL. You had no reason. We shared Ambrose's heart. I never took part of it that was not mine. Do you think we could be friends? . . . no—it is too early to wonder about that. When I return to Florence next week, perhaps we shall know.

PHILIP. You are going back next week?

RACHEL. Yes.

PHILIP. There is no need to hurry.

RACHEL. Ah, but there is. My mission here will be accomplished and I have much to do in Florence. I have to sell the villa alas.

PHILIP. Must you? Why?

RACHEL. I can no longer afford to keep it up.

15

PHILIP. I see.

RACHEL. Let's not talk about unpleasant things. Perhaps you would ring the bell? Seecombe will have prepared the tisane tray the way I showed him by this time. (*Philip pulls a bell rope.*) When Ambrose and I were first married he used to drink brandy in the evening, but I soon changed that.

PHILIP. What is tisane?

RACHEL. There are all kinds. It is a tea made with herbs. I make mine from a receipt given me by my mother. It soothes the nerves and helps you sleep. All through his illness Ambrose could take it when he could take nothing else. (*Seecombe enters with a silver tray, with a tea pot, cups, hot water, etc.*) Thank you, Seecombe. (*Seecombe places the tray on a table by her side.*)

PHILIP. Where on earth did that tray come from, Seecombe?

SEECOMBE. (*Coldly.*) There is a great deal of silver in the family, Mr. Philip. Will that be all, madam?

RACHEL. Yes, thank you, Seecombe. Goodnight.

SEECOMBE. Goodnight, madam. Goodnight, Mr. Philip. (*He goes out with dignity. Rachel giggles.*)

RACHEL. You were snubbed. And rightly. (*She busies herself with the tray.*) Toworrow is Sunday?

PHILIP. Yes.

RACHEL. Ambrose told me of the great box pew you had, and how naughty little Philip used to let mice loose in it.

PHILIP. Following naughty old Ambrose's example.

RACHEL. What a couple of children. Here. (*She hands him a cup.*) Try it. (*He sips.*)

PHILIP It's . . . it's a little bitter.

RACHEL. The next sip will taste less bitter (*She pours a cup for herself.*) I suppose we shall have to go to church.

PHILIP. (*Surprised.*) You wish to?

RACHEL. Ambrose would have wished me to. I am a Catholic, but I will be able to follow the service, I think.

PHILIP. You will create a sensation in Barton.

RACHEL. And after church, Mr. Kendall and his daughter, Louise, come to dine—is that not so?

PHILIP. You know everything.

RACHEL. Miss Louise and you are great friends. She is very pretty, Ambrose said.

PHILIP. She's all right.

16

RACHEL. You are not very gall*ant*, but perhaps Cornwall is full of pretty girls.

PHILIP. Perhaps. I've always been too busy to bother about things like that.

RACHEL. You will not always be too busy. (*She puts down her cup and rises.*) Good night, Philip, and thank you.

PHILIP. Thank me—for what?

RACHEL. Making me welcome in your home.

PHILIP. Must you go—it's early.

RACHEL. I am not a late bird like you and Ambrose. And I am tired. Coming here to Barton for the first time was a slight effort—thank you for making it so easy. Goodnight, Cousin Philip.

PHILIP. Goodnight, Cousin Rachel. (*She picks up the candle and goes slowly up the stairs. She goes into her room, shutting the door behind her.*)

FADE OUT

FADE UP

ACT ONE

Scene 4

It is a sunny morning.
Seecombe bustles in and goes to a cupboard in the alcove which he opens to take out wine glasses. He is followed by James carrying another tray with two decanters of port and madeira. Seecombe has brought in with him a silver dish with ratafia biscuits which he has put on the end of the table.

SEECOMBE. Careful with them now; they've only just seen the light o'day—! (*James lowers the tray on to the sideboard. He sees the dish of biscuits and picks it up curiously.*)

JAMES. What're they?

SEECOMBE. You put them back now, this instant.

JAMES. But what are they?

SEECOMBE. Comfits— (*James looks blank.*)

JAMES. What d'you do with 'em?

SEECOMBE. You eat 'em. (*Blank look of acknowledgment from James.*) Sweet-meats—they're taken with your sherry-madeira-wine and such. Leastways that's what madam says you do wi' 'em.

JAMES. Queer folk the gentry. Now what I fancies is a good mug of ale and— (*There is laughter from beyond the door to the dining room* D.R.)

SEECOMBE. Never you mind: you make yerself scarce—they're comin' through. (*He goes out. As he does so James takes one of the biscuits and darts out. Rachel enters with Kendall.*)

KENDALL. Besides which, m'dear all the congregation, indeed most of the country, know that you came from outlandish foreign parts. For all they know Italians may be black. So many people asked me when they will have an opportunity to meet you— officially. I think you can reckon upon engagements every afternoon for at least the next four weeks.

RACHEL. There is nothing that I would like better, Mr. Kendall, but, alas I am only a visitor to Barton and, in the circumstances . . . (*Louise and Philip enter. After a brief moment Rachel joins Louise.*) Miss Kendall I believe I owe you an apology. Yesterday in my enthusiasm for becoming acquainted with Barton, I unwittingly prevented Philip from calling upon you at Pelyn.

LOUISE. No matter. He had no serious obligation in that respect.

KENDALL. Philip, your cousin should, by rights undertake certain social commitments as she is in this part ot the world. I know that you—and Ambrose paid little heed to such niceties—but I am sure many people in the country would be honoured to meet your cousin Rachel.

PHILIP. (*Smiles as he hands her sherry.*) They would indeed be honoured.

RACHEL. As I say I am merely a visitor and, in the circumstances, I feel I should leave in the morning.

KENDALL. So soon? You're hardly an ordinary visitor, m'dear . . . and had Ambrose lived Barton would have been your home.

RACHEL. Had Ambrose lived, Mr. Kendall, a lot of things would have been otherwise. (*Pause. She changes the conversation deliberately.*) Did you know that Ambrose had planned a sunken garden with a fountain—like the one we had at the villa.

KENDALL. Charming—where was it to be?

RACHEL. I'll show you . . . will you come with me. (*She picks up a shawl and she and Kendall go towards the door.*) We had planned it down to the last detail. It was to have the first thing we were going to do when we came back.

KENDALL. I envy you gardeners your patience. To plant a tree and wait perhaps for years for it to bear fruit.

RACHEL. Ah, but when it does bear fruit—it is worth the waiting. (*They go out.*)

LOUISE. *I'm* waiting, Phil.

PHILIP. What for?

LOUISE. What for?

PHILIP. Oh you mean yesterday afternoon. I'm sorry but it was impossible to get away. My cousin Rachel wished to see all the Barton acres.

LOUISE. Oh, don't apologise. I waited about two hours, but it didn't matter.

PHILIP. I'm really very sorry.

LOUISE. I guessed something of the sort had kept you. I'm thankful it was nothing more serious. I thought you might have had some terrible disagreement.

PHILIP. No. We didn't.

LOUISE. Have you really survived so far without a clash? Tell me all.

PHILIP. What do you mean by all?

LOUISE. What did you say to her? How did she take it? Was she very much aghast by all you said, or did she show no sign of guilt at all?

PHILIP. We've really had little time for talking but she is a very different person from the person I expected. You must have seen that from your brief meeting before the service.

LOUISE. She is very beautiful.

PHILIP. Beautiful?

LOUISE. Yes, beautiful! Ask father. Ask anyone. Didn't you notice how the people stared in Church when she put up her veil?

PHILIP. Of course they stared at her. There hsan't been a woman in the Ashley pew for over thirty years.

LOUISE. Her profile is like that on a rare old coin. She makes the rest of us look like country bumpkins—or bumkinesses—if there is such a word. Has she said much about Ambrose?

PHILIP. Naturally.

LOUISE. What?

PHILIP. Ambrose told her everything.

LOUISE. But those letters . . . I thought . . .

PHILIP. (*Hurriedly.*) We must remember they were written when he was very ill. (*Pause.*)

LOUISE. (*Slowly.*) It's not true.

PHILIP. What isn't?

LOUISE. You can't have changed overnight.

PHILIP. I don't know what you're talking about.

LOUISE. Don't you remember what you said about her last week?

PHILIP. Of course I do; it's just that I might have been a trifle hasty. One must give her the benefit of the doubt. (*Pause.*)

LOUISE. You're fallen in love with her.

PHILIP. Don't be absurd.

LOUISE. It's the only explanation.

PHILIP. I have *not* fallen in love with her. The thing's ridiculous. She only arrived yesterday.

LOUISE. What about Romeo and Juliet?

PHILIP. What about them?

LOUISE. "Whoever loved that loved not at first sight" . . .

PHILIP. That's schoolgirl nonsense.

LOUISE. It isn't—it's Shakespeare. I suppose it's understandable, really. You've never seen a beautiful woman before.

PHILIP. Oh, do stop about her being beautiful.

LOUISE. I never thought I'd watch you making a fool of yourself over a woman years too old for you.

PHILIP. She's not old.

LOUISE. She's thirty-five at least.

PHILIP. For God's sake, Louise, let's talk about something else.

LOUISE. Very well. (*Pause.*) You'll be coming as usual to drive me over to Pascoes tomorrow?

PHILIP. I'm sorry. I can't.

LOUISE. But why? It's all arranged.

PHILIP. I just can't, that's why.

LOUISE. You're going somewhere with her.

PHILIP. If you must know—I'm showing her round the village.

LOUISE. Were you planning to let me know—or were you once more just not going to turn up?

PHILIP. Of course I was going to let you know.

LOUISE. I don't believe you.

PHILIP. All right—don't.

LOUISE. When is she going back to Italy?

PHILIP. I don't know.

20

LOUISE. The sooner the better if you ask me.

PHILIP. I didn't ask you.

LOUISE. (*Brokenly.*) Oh . . . Phil . . .

PHILIP. What on earth's the matter with you, Louise? You're making a stupid scene over nothing, mountains out of molehills or some such . . . and now you're crying.

LOUISE. I am *not.*

PHILIP. All because I said I might have been mistaken about my cousin Rachel.

LOUISE. If you go on talking about her I shall scream.

PHILIP. All right, scream. And I am not the one who's talking about her. You are.

LOUISE. Phil, listen to me . . . (*Voices Offstage. Louise turns away. Kendall and Rachel re-enter.*)

KENDALL. My dear Philip, I think this sunken garden is a splendid idea. One very important thing about it. though—we must persuade Mrs. Ashley to stay on for a while and at least see it started.

RACHEL. I'm afraid that may not be possible.

KENDALL. Try and persuade your cousin, Philip.

PHILIP. I'll do my best, sir.

LOUISE. It's time we were going, Father.

KENDALL. No hurry, my dear. Tell me, Mrs. Ashley, do you not think there is a remarkable resemblance between Philip and Ambrose?

RACHEL. When I first saw Cousin Philip, I thought he *was* Ambrose.

KENDALL. All the Ashleys bear a strong family likeness.

RACHEL. My father had the unmistakeable nose.

KENDALL. Ambrose used to say it was the ideal nose for looking down.

RACHEL. Philip—when we go through Ambrose's books, there may be some that Mr. Kendall might like.

PHILIP. Good idea. And I'd like you to have his walking stick, sir. You've brought it, Cousin Rachel?

RACHEL. I've brought everything, even to the battered old hat he used to wear in the garden. I brought that specially for you, Philip.

LOUISE. (*Abruptly.*) Father, I've got a bad headache.

KENDALL. Have you, dear? I'm sorry. Well, we'd better be getting home. Now, Mrs. Ashley, please arrange with Philip what evening you can come to dinner and let us know. We're free every evening except Monday, are we not, Louise?

LOUISE. Yes, Father. ·

KENDALL. Well, goodbye, Mrs. Ashley, it's been delightful. And no more of this nonsense about hurrying back to Italy. Now you're here we're going to keep you for a while. Goodbye, Philip.

PHILIP. Goodbye, sir.

LOUISE. Goodbye, Mrs. Ashley.

RACHEL. Goodbye, Miss Kendall. I look forward to dining with you very much.

KENDALL. Perhaps we can fix a day now.

RACHEL. Would Tuesday be convenient? Oh no—I forgot Philip always goes over to Lydstone on Tuesdays. Wednesday perhaps?

KENDALL. Capital—eh, Louise?

LOUISE. Yes, Father.

RACHEL. Philip?

PHILIP. Fine.

KENDALL. Very well. Till Wednesday. Come, my dear. (*They go out accompanied by Philip. Rachel moves about tidying the cushions. Philip returns from the door.*)

RACHEL. I'm sorry your Miss Kendall had a headache.

PHILIP. Yes—and she's not my Miss Kendall.

RACHEL. Oh? I thought from something that Ambrose once said . . .

PHILIP. What?

RACHEL. Never mind. Philip, as I may be leaving soon, don't you think it would be a good idea to go through Ambrose's things?

PHILIP. I'll tell Seecombe to get the trunks brought down. (*He goes to the door and calls.*) Seecombe!

SEECOMBE. (*Offstage.*) Yes, Mr. Philip.

PHILIP. Get Mr. Ambrose's trunks brought down, will you?

SEECOMBE. (*Offstage.*) Yes, Mr. Philip. (*Philip returns. Rachel has been wandering around. She turns and smiles at him.*)

RACHEL. I can see this is a bachelor establishment. Not a single mirror except in the bedrooms—and then only tiny ones, set at the most uncomfortable angles.

PHILIP. Cousin Rachel?

RACHEL. Yes?

PHILIP. Could you not be persuaded to stay on a little and, as Uncle Nick mentioned, just get the sunken garden started.

RACHEL. I shall have to think about it.

PHILIP. I wish you would.

RACHEL. The trouble is I really must see Signor Rainaldi about selling the villa.

PHILIP. Could you not write to him?

RACHEL. Possibly, but I would like to be there. Imagine if it were Barton that was to be sold. The villa is my home.

PHILIP. Barton is your home.

RACHEL. You're very sweet, Philip, and very kind . . . (*Noise Offstage. Seecombe and James, appear from the servants' quarters, lugging two large trunks.*)

PHILIP. Here by the fire, Seecombe.

SEECOMBE. Right you are, Mr. Philip, sir.

RACHEL. Oh, Seecombe, would you bring me the Tisane tray about five?

SEECOMBE. Very good, madam.

RACHEL. I'm going to cure Mr. Philip of drinking India tea in the afternoon.

SEECOMBE. Very good, madam. (*Seecombe goes off with James.*)

RACHEL. Shall we have a look at the books first? (*Philip undoes the clasp on the first trunk and throws back the lid. Rachel kneels down in front of the trunk and starts to sort the books.*) "Your Gardening Companion," "Tuscan Gardens," "Gardens of Northern Italy" . . . "The Flowers of Florence"—I'd forgotten how many gardening books we had acquired . . . "Herbs and their Uses" . . . I'll give this one to you, Philip, so that you can make yourself tisane after I've gone . . . Shakespeare, a lovely edition. Mr. Kendall would appreciate that, don't you think? More books about gardening . . . ah! "The Sunken Garden," that will be useful if you decide.

PHILIP. (*Interrupting.*) I have decided. We're having the sunken garden.

RACHEL. Poetry . . . Lord Byron, Shelley, Keats . . . Ambrose loved the poetry of Keats . . . "In some melodious plot, Of beechen green and shadows numberless, Singest of summer in full-throated ease . . ." Andrew Marvell . . . "Annihilating all that's made to a green thought in a green shade . . ." That's what we'll have in that sunken garden, Philip, "a green thought in a green shade" . . . more and more gardening books. Here—take your book and the book for Mr. Kendall. I'll go through the gardening books on my own some time. I don't know which are worth keeping—they deal mostly with Italian gardens. (*She rises and hands the two books to Philip, then shuts the lid of the trunk. Philip undoes the second trunk and throws back the lid. Rachel begins to look inside, then suddenly sways and puts her hand to her eyes.*)

PHILIP. Cousin Rachel! (*She sways against him. He puts his arm around her.*)

RACHEL. I'm sorry.

PHILIP. Here, come and sit down.

RACHEL. No—no, I'll be all right.

PHILIP. We'll finish this another time.

RACHEL. No. (*She draws away from him, pulls herself together and kneels down by the trunk. She lifts out a jacket.*) For you?

PHILIP. I couldn't.

RACHEL. It was his favourite jacket . . . I can see him now—sitting by the fountain . . .

PHILIP. Please, Rachel, let's leave this for another time.

RACHEL. No, let's get it over. I'd no idea that clothes could be so cruel. What shall we do with them?

PHILIP. Seecombe might have a suggestion—he's a wise old bird.

RACHEL. Yes. (*She reaches into the trunk and produces a battered old hat.*) This?

PHILIP. Yes, that I will have. (*He takes it and crosses to the door. He calls.*) Seecombe!

RACHEL. Do you never ring for him?

PHILIP. Sometimes. Usually Ambrose and I just shouted. (*Seecombe enters.*) Seecombe, we'd like your advice—Mr. Ambrose's clothes, what shall we do with them.

SEECOMBE. They'd fit you, sir.

PHILIP. No, Seecombe.

SEECOMBE. I see. Well, Mr. Philip, sir, what about giving them round to the servants and the men on the estate? Christmas is coming and the clothes could be a bonus on top of their usual presents.

PHILIP. I knew I could rely on you, Seecombe.

SEECOMBE. Yes, sir. Shall I have the trunks removed, sir?

PHILIP. Yes, put that one in the library.

SEECOMBE. Yes, sir. (*To Rachel.*) You look tired, madam. Shall I bring in the tray?

RACHEL. Please. (*Seecombe goes out.*) Dear Seecombe . . . he understands.

PHILIP. Yes.

RACHEL. The clothes brought him back so vividly. I remember

when I first met him at a dinner party given by the Contessa di Paoli. It was one of those typical Florentine occasions with everyone talking their heads off. He sat on my right and looked— oh so desperately bored. I hadn't heard his name properly and tried, unsuccessfully, to find a topic of conversation that might interest him. He was polite but gave no help. Finally, I asked him what part of England he came from and he said Cornwall. I said I had Cornish blood and that my maiden name had been Ashley. He looked at me as if he saw me for the first time and said . . . "You must be my Cousin Rachel" . . . "I am Ambrose Ashley." (*Seecombe enters with the tisane tray. Rachel smiles her thanks and as Seecombe goes out she begins to prepare the tea.*) I asked him what he was doing in Florence and he told me he had come for his health as the Cornish winter tried him sorely and to look at the gardens. "Then you must look at my garden at the Villa Sangaletti," I said, and we arranged that he should call the following morning. Then the hostess rose and we had no further opportunity of further speech. But he came early the next morning and I showed him over my garden . . . he was so enthusiastic and so knowledgable. Then we sat and drank tisane just as you and I are doing, there in the sunlight. I felt a sense of well being and happiness—I'd never known before. My first marriage had been unfortunate. Guido was so much older than I, cold and unfeeling, aloof and completely without compassion, whereas Ambrose was so warm, so understanding. I think we both knew that first morning. I know I did. After he had gone I sat on as if in a dream—a dream that was soon to become a wonderful reality. (*She puts down her cup.*) I talk too much.

PHILIP. No.

RACHEL. It is a great thing to be able to say—"Then I was happy." Another cup?

PHILIP. Thank you.

RACHEL. Ah, it does not taste so bitter now. (*She smiles at him.*)

PHILIP. Louise was right—you are beautiful.

RACHEL. Am I?

PHILIP. Very Beautiful.

RACHEL. I am thirty-five, Philip.

PHILIP. Really? I thought you were older.

RACHEL. From you I take that as a compliment.

PHILIP. Might I ask you something?

RACHEL. Of course—anything.

PHILIP. Do you really have to sell your villa?

RACHEL. Yes.

PHILIP. I wish . . .

RACHEL. Yes . . . ?

PHILIP. Uncle Nick was surprised that Ambrose had not made another will—in your favour.

RACHEL. Ah—but he did.

PHILIP. He did?

RACHEL. It was never signed.

PHILIP. Why?

RACHEL. He was ill. Do you mind if we do not talk about it, Philip?

PHILIP. But we *must* talk about it.

RACHEL. No!

PHILIP. I say we must.

RACHEL. Then I shall go to my room.

PHILIP. No.

RACHEL. If you insist—I shall return to Italy tomorrow.

PHILIP. But why? Why will you not talk about it?

RACHEL. I am a woman. I have my reasons. I am a very private person. I must ask you to respect that privacy.

PHILIP. If it is simply a matter of money . . .

RACHEL. Money? One can always get money somehow. I could pawn my rings . . . or live in London and give lessons in Italian.

PHILIP. Mrs. Ambrose Ashley give lessons in Italian!

RACHEL. I have no false pride, Philip . . . good night.

PHILIP. Don't go!

RACHEL. You leave me no choice.

PHILIP. I won't mention it again—only—don't go!

RACHEL. I would prefer to if you don't mind. I am suddenly very tired. It was foolish of me to insist on going through Ambrose's things . . . inanimate objects can hurt so much.

PHILIP. I am dreadfully sorry. Please forgive me.

RACHEL. Of course. There is nothing to forgive. Good night. (*She goes slowly upstairs and into her room. The door closes. Philip swears and kicks the logs of the fire. Seecombe enters.*)

SEECOMBE. May I remove the tray, sir?

PHILIP. Yes. (*There is a ring at the front door.*) Who the hell . . . ? (*Seecombe goes to the door and admits Kendall.*) Uncle Nick!

KENDALL. Left my spectacles behind—blind as a bat without them.

PHILIP. Where did you have them last?

KENDALL. When I came back from the garden with Mrs. Ashley.

PHILIP. Look for them, Seecombe, will you? Uncle Nick—this is providential. I must have a word with you.

KENDALL. Where's Mrs. Ashley?

PHILIP. Gone to her room.

KENDALL. A bit early, isn't it?

PHILIP. She was tired.

SEECOMBE. Here are your spectacles, sir.

KENDALL. Thank you, Seecombe. (*Seecombe goes out.*) Well, Philip, in my opinion, Mrs. Ashley is a fine woman. I commend Ambrose's taste. Changed your opinion, I hope.

PHILIP. He did make another will.

KENDALL. Who did?

PHILIP. Ambrose.

KENDALL. How do you know?

PHILIP. She told me. I asked her. He never signed it.

KENDALL. Why not?

PHILIP. He was ill, she said.

KENDALL. Do you know the terms?

PHILIP. She didn't tell me.

KENDALL. Extraordinary!

PHILIP. I tried to insist but she became angry. Finally she said she could always pawn her rings and give Italian lessons.

KENDALL. We can't allow that.

PHILIP. Of course not.

KENDALL. Why didn't he sign it? Ambrose was always so business like.

PHILIP. What can we do?

KENDALL. Make her an allowance from the estate.

PHILIP. Would she accept it?

KENDALL. We can but try.

PHILIP. How much?

KENDALL. Up to you, my boy.

PHILIP. Two hundred pounds a quarter?

KENDALL. That's generous—but why not?

PHILIP. Will you see about it at once?

KENDALL. I'll send my boy over with the deed tomorrow. Italian lessons—eh!

PHILIP. A glass of brandy?

KENDALL. Thank you. (*Philip crosses and pours two brandies.*) Most extraordinary. (*Both drink.*) Well, Philip, in a few months you'll be monarch of all you survey.

PHILIP. On All Fools Day. What a day to choose for a birthday.

KENDALL. And my duties cease.

PHILIP. You've been the best guardian a fellow ever had.

KENDALL. Funny—Ambrose insisting you wait till you were twenty-five.

PHILIP. He always said a man didn't know his own mind till twenty-five and no woman until she was thirty.

KENDALL. Women know their own minds in the cradle.

PHILIP. Really, Uncle Nick!

KENDALL. But then you and Ambrose never knew the first thing about women. That's why I'm so glad . . .

PHILIP. Yes?

KENDALL. That Mrs. Ashley seems such an exceptional woman.

PHILIP. Yes.

KENDALL. Ambrose could so easily have fallen a prey to the wrong sort . . . remarkable eyes.

PHILIP. Yes.

KENDALL. That's the Italian blood of course.

PHILIP. Yes.

KENDALL. I'm surprised that Ambrose never sent for any of the Ashley jewelery.

PHILIP. I'd forgotten about the jewels—very fine some of them I believe?

KENDALL. They're magnificent. Your grandfather was a great collector—the emeralds alone are superb.

PHILIP. I seem to remember a famous pearl collar . . .

KENDALL. It's the gem of the whole lot in my opinion. Well, I must be going . . . I'll get that sent round tomorrow.

PHILIP. Good.

KENDALL. (*Going to the door.*) Louise seems a little under the weather, poor child . . . (*Philip remains silent.*) well, see you on Wednesday—and do give my regards to Mrs. Ashley.

PHILIP. I will. Goodnight, Uncle Nick, and thank you. (*Kendall goes out. Philip escorts him then returns to the room and stands for a moment in thought. Then he runs up the stairs and taps at Rachel's door.*)

RACHEL. (*Offstage.*) Who is it?

PHILIP. Philip. (*Pause. Then slowly the door opens and Rachel appears, her hair is down and she wears a wrap.*)

RACHEL. Yes, Philip?

PHILIP. I . . . I . . .

RACHEL. Why do you stare at me like that?

PHILIP. I've never seen a woman in undress before.

RACHEL. (*Smiling.*) What was it you wanted?

PHILIP. I just hoped you weren't cross with me—that's all.

RACHEL. No, Philip, I'm not cross with you. (*She leans forward and kisses him on the cheek, then quickly shuts the door. Philip stands for a moment and then gleefully bounds down the stairs, smiling happily.*)

FADE OUT

FADE UP

ACT ONE

SCENE 5

It is next day. Late afternoon.
The bell rings at the front door. Seecombe emerges and admits Kendall.

KENDALL. Mr. Philip in?

SEECOMBE. Yes, sir. Just back from riding, sir. I'll let him know you're here.

KENDALL. Thank you. (*Seecombe goes upstairs and off. Kendall takes a document and studies it. Seecombe reappears upstairs.*)

SEECOMBE. (*Descending.*) Will you take a glass of wine, sir? Mr. Philip won't be a moment.

KENDALL. No, thank you, Seecombe. (*As Seecombe exits, Philip appears upstairs.*)

PHILIP. (*Descending.*) Hallo, Uncle Nick.

KENDALL. Thought I'd bring this over myself. (*He hands the document to Philip who reads it quickly and hands it back.*)

PHILIP. Thank you. Yes. Very well put.

KENDALL. How is Mrs. Ashley?

PHILIP. Fine. We've been out riding.

KENDALL. I thought it might be a good idea if I had a word with her (*Indicating the deed.*) about this.

PHILIP. Oh?

KENDALL. I thought the reason why she refused to disclose the terms of the unsigned will might be—er—reasons of delicacy—you being the heir.

PHILIP. I see . . .

29

KENDALL. She might talk to me more freely.

PHILIP. Shall I call her?

KENDALL. If you would.

PHILIP. And then vanish. Is that the idea?

KENDALL. Precisely.

PHILIP. Right. (*He goes upstairs and knocks at Rachel's door.*) Cousin Rachel . . .

RACHEL. (*Offstage.*) Yes?

PHILIP. Uncle Nick is here. He'd like a word with you.

RACHEL. (*Offstage.*) Of course. (*Philip makes a thumbs-up gesture to Kendall and goes off upstairs. Pause. Rachel emerges from her room and comes down the stairs.*) Mr. Kendall—what a pleasant surprise.

KENDALL. I hear you have been out riding.

RACHEL. Yes. What a beautiful part of the world. I am more than ever proud of my Cornish blood.

KENDALL. Mrs. Ashley—I had a talk with Philip yesterday.

RACHEL. Oh yes? Won't you sit down?

KENDALL. Thank you. Mrs. Ashley, Philip and I wish you to do Barton a favour . . .

RACHEL. But of course. I have already promised to give away prizes at the Harvest Festival.

KENDALL. Perhaps you would be so kind as to glance at this? (*He hands her a document which she reads quickly.*)

RACHEL. Mr. Kendall . . . (*She puts her hands across her eyes.*)

KENDALL. It's the least Barton can do for you.

RACHEL. I won't deny it will be very welcome. My first husband left me such a legacy of debt. I am most grateful to Philip—and to you.

KENDALL. If Ambrose had signed the other will . . .

RACHEL. So Philip told you . . .

KENDALL. Yes.

RACHEL. I'm afraid I was—not as kind to him as I should have been. I was . . . well . . . I was embarrassed.

KENDALL. Perfectly understandable, dear lady, perfectly.

RACHEL. Thank you.

KENDALL. He had left you everything?

RACHEL. For my lifetime or until I remarried . . . then to Philip and his heirs.

KENDALL. I see.

RACHEL. Now let us talk of something else. How is your daughter's headache?

KENDALL. Much better.

RACHEL. She's a very pretty girl.

KENDALL. I think so.

RACHEL. Everyone must think so. She'd be a sensation in Florence with her delicate English coloring. (*Seecombe appears.*)

SEECOMBE. Shall I bring in the tray, madam?

RACHEL. Please do, Seecombe. And call Mr. Philip—you'll stay, will you not, Mr. Kendall?

KENDALL. Seecombe offered me a glass of sherry earlier.

RACHEL. I'll pour it for you. (*She pours the wine. During the next few lines, Seecombe goes up stairs to call Philip, then descends and goes off to get the tray.*) I have never been to a Harvest Festival.

KENDALL. It's quite an occasion here. The tense rivalry about who has grown the largest pumpkin . . .

RACHEL. I do not think we have them in Italy.

KENDALL. I'm glad you have promised to give away the prizes. The Festival is still a month away, so you will not be leaving Barton immediately.

RACHEL. The temptation to stay for a little and start the sunken garden is, I admit, very great.

KENDALL. Good! I hope it may prove overwhelming. (*Philip appears and begins to come down the stairs. Rachel meets him at the foot.*)

RACHEL. Philip . . . my dear Philip . . . what a sweet and generous gesture.

PHILIP. Oh, it's nothing.

RACHEL. It is a great deal. (*She presses his arm and turns back to Kendall.*)

KENDALL. I think we are going to win, Philip.

PHILIP. Oh?

KENDALL. The temptation to stay and start the sunken garden is proving too strong for Mrs. Ashley.

PHILIP. Splendid. (*Seecombe appears with the tray and brings it to Rachel.*)

RACHEL. Thank you, Seecombe. Yes, I am weakening. How long do you think it would take, Philip?

PHILIP. Could my estate men manage, do you think, or should we need to call in experts?

RACHEL. Your head gardener Tamlyn is very good. I think if he and I drew up the plans we could manage with the under-gardeners and the men from the estate.

PHILIP. It would take several months. The days are beginning to draw in.

RACHEL. Perhaps if I stayed until Christmas . . .

KENDALL. Capital. Barton Christmases are quite occasions.

RACHEL. And then perhaps came back in the Spring?

KENDALL. And the sunken garden should be ready for Philip's coming of age in April. I'll drink to that. (*He does so. Rachel hands Philip a cup of tisane.*)

RACHEL. You are having a big celebration?

PHILIP. No. The celebrations will be at Christmas.

RACHEL. I shall look forward to Christmas.

KENDALL. (*Suddenly.*) Isn't this pleasant? You know, Mrs. Ashley, you supply the one ingredient needed to make Barton ideal.

RACHEL. And what is that?

KENDALL. A woman. Do you not agree, Philip?

PHILIP. Certainly.

RACHEL. You are very charming, both of you.

KENDALL. A house is not a home without a woman.

RACHEL. You are fortunate in having a daughter.

KENDALL. Louise is a child still—completely absorbed in her dogs and horses. Do you hunt, Mrs. Ashley?

RACHEL. I'm afraid not.

KENDALL. We must see about that. I have a mare that might suit you.

PHILIP. My cousin found Dolabella much to her liking.

KENDALL. Dear old Dolabella . . . still, she must try my Angelica.

PHILIP. I think we could provide Mrs. Ashley with something suitable.

KENDALL. No doubt, no doubt.

PHILIP. I've been thinking of buying some new hunters.

KENDALL. The price of a good hunter is staggering these days.

PHILIP. My cousin Rachel needs a horse that she likes and likes her. I'm sure you'll agree to that.

KENDALL. That is why I suggested Angelica. She's as gentle as a lamb. (*Rachel is quietly amused by this exchange. She watches covertly over her teacup.*)

PHILIP. Angelica is past it, Uncle Nick.

KENDALL. Nonsense . . . now your Dolabella . . . (*He is interrupted by Seecombe entering with letters on a salver.*)

SEECOMBE. The post has come, Mr. Philip.(*Philip takes the letters from the salver.*)

PHILIP. Thank you, Seecombe.

SEECOMBE. Have you finished, madam?

RACHEL. Yes. You may take the tray.

SEECOMBE. Thank you, madam. (*Seecombe takes the tray. Philip hands two letters to Rachel.*)

PHILIP. Two for you—from Italy.

RACHEL. Ah—from my faithful Signor Rainaldi. (*She rises.*) If you will forgive me. These letters will probably need my immediate attention. Goodbye, Mr. Kendall and thank you.

PHILIP. Dinner will be in half an hour.

RACHEL. I am not likely to forget. Seecombe told me we are having guinea fowl—a particular favourite of mine—and of Ambrose. (*She goes upstairs.*)

KENDALL. Delightful woman.

PHILIP. What can he be writing about?

KENDALL. Who? Signor Rainaldi? Business, I suppose.

PHILIP. I couldn't stand the fellow. I expect he's trying to get her to go back to Florence.

KENDALL. Well—she's staying here until Christmas at any rate. No more of this talk of going to London and giving Italian lessons.

PHILIP. No,.thank God!

KENDALL. I have promised Louise to take her up to London before Christmas. She will stay with an old school friend.

PHILIP. Did she tell you about the will?

KENDALL. Yes. I was right. It was a matter of delicacy. Ambrose had left her everything for her lifetime.

PHILIP. I see.

KENDALL. Or until she remarried.

PHILIP. She's not likely to do that.

KENDALL. Why not? An attractive woman like that? She's not likely to remain a widow long.

PHILIP. She was devoted to Ambrose.

KENDALL. My dear Philip—however devoted one may have been to one's partner—and I was devoted to my dear Alison, there comes a time . . . however, we shall see. Well, I must be going. Any message for Louise?

PHILIP. Oh, the usual—looking forward to seeing her and all that.

KENDALL. What a casual generation you are. Now, in my day—well, goodbye, my boy.

PHILIP. Goodbye, Uncle Nick.

KENDALL. (*Going.*) I should forget that Dolabella if I were you—Angelica is just what Mrs. Ashley needs. (*He goes off. Philip stands looking after him for a moment.*)

PHILIP. (*Calling.*) Seecombe! (*Seecombe appears from the kitchen regions.*)

SEECOMBE. Mr. Philip?

PHILIP. Tell George to bring Cyprian round in the morning. I am going to ride into Bodmin. I hear that old Stebbins has some promising young hunters.

SEECOMBE. Very good, Mr. Philip.

PHILIP. Oh and Seecombe—a bottle of the best claret with dinner. Better decant it now and have another one ready.

SEECOMBE. Very good, Mr. Philip.

PHILIP. By the way, Seecombe. Mrs. Ashley has decided to stay on for a bit—at least until Christmas.

SEECOMBE. That is excellent news, Mr. Philip. If I may make so bold, sir, madam has made a great impression in the servants' Hall.

PHILIP. I'm sure she has.

SEECOMBE. We are all agreed, sir, that a mistress has been needed at Barton for a long time.

PHILIP. (*Quoting.*) "A house is not a home without a woman" . . . that's what Mr. Kendall said.

SEECOMBE. Mr. Kendall should know, sir, he's been a widower these ten years. When Miss Louise marries, he'll find himself very lonely. Will that be all, sir?

PHILIP. Yes, Seecombe, that will be all. (*Seecombe goes . . . leaving Philip scowling.*) Uncle Nick . . .

FADE DOWN

FADE UP

ACT ONE

Scene 6

James is struggling with a Christmas tree in a tub, to get it into position, downstairs. Seecombe supervises.

SEECOMBE. James, the fourth branch on the right is bent. (*James, none too sure of his arithmetic, points to each branch in turn as Seecombe counts to him.*) One—two—three—four! Yes, that one. Raise it a touch. Gently, boy, gently! The tree must seem to be standing as nature placed it. Oh, and do be careful not to stamp on the berries . . .

JAMES. Sorry Mr. Seecombe, sir.

SEECOMBE. Now leave it. Come away. Right away, One further movement and the whole effect is spoiled. My! That's beautiful! Now, boy, the dinner will start as usual at five o'clock. The trestles are already up and laid?

JAMES. Yes, Mr. Seecombe, sir.

SEECOMBE. Then here's the seating order. (*And he hands him a list and pile of cards.*)

JAMES. What do I do with these?

SEECOMBE. The names of all the guests are on those pieces of paper, boy. You just place them on the appropriate platters.

JAMES. But you forget, Mr. Seecombe, there are folks as can't read.

SEECOMBE. I forget nothing, James. I have made quite certain that those who can't read have neighbours who can. Now just do as you are told and put them on the appropriate platters.

JAMES. But you forget, Mr. Seecombe, I'm one of them as can't read.

SEECOMBE. Oh damn you, boy. Give them there. I'll do it myself. (*James rushes off and Philip enters.*)

PHILIP. That's a fine tree, Seecombe.

SEECOMBE. Glad you like it, Mr. Philip.

PHILIP. Where's the mistress?

SEECOMBE. Madam is in the kitchen, sir. Cook is a trifle behind, I'm afraid.

PHILIP. Have they started to arrive yet?

SEECOMBE. Yes, sir. The long barn is filling up already . . . William and Thomas are serving ale—and sweet sherry for the ladies.

PHILIP. How many will we be?

SEECOMBE. About seventy, sir.

PHILIP. A good turn-out!

SEECOMBE. Yes, sir, the whole of Barton.

PHILIP. Excellent! Now, when Mr. Kendall and Miss Louise arrive, we shall have a glass of wine here and when everything is quite ready, will you ring the bell and we'll come along to the barn.

SEECOMBE. Very good, Mr. Philip.

PHILIP. The presents—all organised?

SEECOMBE. Yes, sir, yours and madam's.

PHILIP. Madam's?

SEECOMBE. Madam has arranged a personal gift for everyone on the estate, sir.

PHILIP. Good heavens!

SEECOMBE. Most particular she was that no one should be left out. Madam was—er—good enough to consult me in the matter, sir.

PHILIP. Very wise of her.

SEECOMBE. Quite so, sir. (*Rachel enters from the kitchen. She is laughing.*)

RACHEL. I didn't know there *could* be so many mince-pies. Your tree looks beautiful, Seecombe.

SEECOMBE. Thank you, madam. (*He goes out.*)

PHILIP. You look beautiful, too, Rachel.

RACHEL. Are you implying that I resemble the Christmas tree?

PHILIP. No. Come here—I've something for you.

RACHEL. I hope you haven't been extravagant.

PHILIP. No. The extravagant one was my great great grand-father.

RACHEL. What do you mean?

PHILIP. Shut your eyes.

RACHEL. What *is* the mystery?

PHILIP. Shut your eyes, Rachel. (*She does so. He takes a wonderful pearl collar from his pocket and clasps it round her neck.*) Now you may open them.

RACHEL. Philip—what have you . . . (*She crosses to one of the mirrors which now hang in the hall, looks in it and gasps.*) Philip!

PHILIP. It's the Ashley pearl collar. Quite famous, I believe.

RACHEL. For me?

PHILIP. Who else?

RACHEL. I . . . I don't know what to say.

PHILIP. There's no need to say anything.

RACHEL. It's exquisite. I've always longed for pearls—I've never owned any . . . and now this. Oh, Philip, and all I have for you are these links . . . (*She hands him a small box, which he opens.*)

PHILIP. I shall wear them always.

RACHEL. Such a little thing.

36

PHILIP. They're beautiful.

RACHEL. (*Fingering the collar.*) I feel like a queen.

PHILIP. I'm glad.

RACHEL. The pearls . . . I (*She stops.*)

PHILIP. Yes?

RACHEL. The pearls I have seen—the ones worn by my friends in Florence—were not nearly as fine as these.

PHILIP. My great great grandfather—and yours—knew a great deal about jewelery. The Ashley collection is quite famous.

RACHEL. Where is it? I'd love to see it.

PHILIP. In the bank.

RACHEL. What a pity! Jewels should be worn . . . however, when you marry . . . did you know that if pearls are not worn they die?

PHILIP. No.

RACHEL. I shall not let these die. (*There is the sound of a carriage drawing up.*)

PHILIP. That will be Uncle Nick and Louise. (*He goes to the door. Rachel again goes to the mirror and fingers the pearls.*)

KENDALL. (*Offstage.*) Hello, Philip—Merry Christmas . . .

PHILIP. (*Offstage.*) Merry Christmas, Uncle Nick—Louise . . .

LOUISE. (*Offstage.*) Merry Christmas, Philip. (*They enter. Louise is carrying two parcels.*)

KENDALL. Ah, Mrs. Ashley—Merry Christmas to you. (*His manner to her has changed. It is cold.*)

RACHEL. Merry Christmas, Mr. Kendall, and to you, Miss Louise. (*Louise murmurs something. Both she and Kendall suddenly notice the pearl collar.*) Isn't it beautiful? From Philip.

KENDALL. (*Slowly.*) The Ashley collar. . . .

RACHEL. I've never seen one like it.

KENDALL. No. It's unique.

RACHEL. It has a history!

KENDALL. Yes. Each pearl is perfect, and perfectly matched. They took many years to collect. A famous jeweler at the French Court designed and made it. It is the best thing in the Ashley collection.

RACHEL. I told Philip I did not know how to thank him.

PHILIP. Wear it—that's all I ask. Uncle Nick—Louise, your presents are in the long barn.

LOUISE. These are for you, Mrs. Ashley, and you, Philip. (*She hurriedly thrusts the parcels at Philip.*)

PHILIP. Thank you. We'll put them by the tree. Rachel, I hear that you have presents for everyone on the estate.

RACHEL. Only little things.

PHILIP. It was a very generous thought. Just like you, wasn't it, Uncle Nick?

KENDALL. Yes . . . (*Seecombe enters.*)

SEECOMBE. Excuse me, madam, but cook says would you be so good as to spare her a few moments? Here's your apron, madam.

RACHEL. Of course. Nothing wrong, I hope?

SEECOMBE. No, Madam. I gather it's the matter of the spice in some sauce.

RACHEL. Excuse me. (*Rachel goes out with Seecombe.*)

KENDALL. The Ashley collar . . .

PHILIP. Yes . . . dosen't it suit her?

KENDALL. You got it out of the bank?

PHILIP. Yes. Old Couch was a bit difficult to start with, but I got it.

KENDALL. He had no right to give it to you.

PHILIP. Why not? It's mine.

KENDALL. Not until April 1st.

PHILIP. Really, Uncle Nick . . . sherry?

KENDALL. Thank you. (*Philip pours out drink.*) I'm glad of this opportunity of speaking to you.

PHILIP. You look very grave. Is anything the matter?

KENDALL. I'm afraid so. I've had a letter from Mr. Couch, Philip.

PHILIP. About the collar?

KENDALL. No. When did you get it?

PHILIP. Yesterday.

KENDALL. This was written the day before. As is very right and proper, he believes it his duty to inform me that Mrs. Ashley is several hundred pounds overdrawn on her account.

PHILIP. Oh?

KENDALL. I don't understand it. She can't have many expenses here. She is living as your guest, so her needs are met. The only thing that occurs to me is that she must be sending money out of the country.

PHILIP. There must be some mistake. She is very generous. You heard her say she has given a present to everyone on the estate. That cannot be done for a few shillings.

KENDALL. Fifty pounds would pay for them a dozen times over. They could not account for such a large overdraft.

PHILIP. She has spent money on the house. The Blue Room has new hangings—and about time too.

KENDALL. The fact remains the sum we agreed to pay her quarterly has been trebled, nearly quadrupled by the amount she has drawn. What are we to decide for the future?

PHILIP. Treble, quadruple the amount we give her now.

KENDALL. Philip!

PHILIP. Uncle Nick—it is Christmas Day and we are boring Louise.

KENDALL. A lady of quality living in London could not fritter away so much.

PHILIP. There may be debts of which we know nothing. She may have creditors, pressing her for money, in Florence. I want you to increase her allowance to cover the over-draft.

KENDALL. And the collar?

PHILIP. What of it? No harm can come to it in her keeping.

KENDALL. I am not so sure.

PHILIP. What are you suggesting?

KENDALL. It would fetch a considerable price.

PHILIP. Uncle Nick—if you dare . . .

KENDALL. You know Louise and I have been in London?

PHILIP. If you dare suggest that my cousin Rachel . . .

KENDALL. (*Interrupting.*) Tell him, Louise.

LOUISE. Oh, Father—must I?

KENDALL. Yes, my dear, you must.

LOUISE. Philip . . . when I was in London I stayed with my great friend Vanessa Dudley.

PHILIP. Well?

LOUISE. She and her parents—her father is in the Diplomatic Service—lived in Florence at one time.

PHILIP. And . . .

LOUISE. They heard that Ambrose had married the Contessa Sangaletti.

PHILIP. Go on.

LOUISE. Oh, Philip, I don't want to.

PHILIP. Say what you have to say and have done with it.

LOUISE. Her mother told me that they were horrified. She— Mrs. Ashley, I mean—and her first husband were notorious for their extravagance.

39

KENDALL. Not only for their extravagance. For loose living.

PHILIP. Filthy gossip.

LOUISE. The tradesmen were never paid. She gave enormous parties and wore the most wonderful pearls.

PHILIP. Ah, that proves your friends are liars. She never had any pearls until today. She told me so.

KENDALL. Be that as it may—I must ask you to return the collar. It must be put back in the bank with the rest of the collection.

PHILIP. Return the collar? Impossible! I gave it to her as a Christmas present. It is the last thing in the world I would do.

KENDALL. Then I must speak to her about it.

PHILIP. I'll be damned if you do.

KENDALL. *(Altering his tone.)* Come, Philip, you are very young and very impressionable. I quite understand that you wish to give your cousin a present—but not the Ashley collar.

PHILIP. She has a right to it. If Ambrose had lived . . .

KENDALL. Ah, yes—if Ambrose had lived. But not now. The jewels remain in trust for your wife, Philip. And that is another reason why it must be returned. The collar has a significance of its own which some of the older tenants at dinner today will know about and talk about. An Ashley allows his bride to wear it on her wedding day as her sole adornment. This is just the sort of thing which causes gossip. I am sure Mrs. Ashley would want to avoid such gossip.

PHILIP. Rubbish! *(Rachel appears in the doorway. They do not notice her.)*

KENDALL. Nevertheless that collar must be returned to the bank. I repeat—it is not yours to give—yet. And if you will not ask Mrs. Ashley to return it, then I shall. *(They glare at each other. Rachel comes forward.)*

RACHEL. I am sorry—I could not help overhearing.

KENDALL. Mrs. Ashley . . .

RACHEL. It's perfectly all right, Mr. Kendall. Please do not be embarrassed. It was dear of Philip to let me wear the pearls tonight and quite right of you to ask for their return.

PHILIP. No, Rachel! No! *(She unclasps the pearls and hands them to Kendall.)*

KENDALL. Thank you, Mrs. Ashley. You understand the collar is part of the Trust and Philip had no business to take it from the bank. But young men are headstrong.

RACHEL. Do you need wrapping for it?

KENDALL. Thank you, no. My handkerchief will do. (*He wraps it in his handkerchief and puts it in his pocket. The bell sounds.*)

RACHEL. Ah, all is ready. Shall we go in?

PHILIP. Uncle Nick—will you go on in with Louise. I wish to speak with my Cousin Rachel. (*Kendall bows. Louise takes his arm and they go off.*) God damn him and send him to hell! ·

RACHEL. Hush. You mustn't say such things.

PHILIP. I wanted you to wear it. I wanted you to keep it always.

RACHEL. I am very proud to have worn it this once.

PHILIP. He's ruined it all, all I had planned.

RACHEL. You're behaving like a child, Philip.

PHILIP. I'm twenty-five all but three blasted months. Don't you know why I wanted you to wear the collar?

RACHEL. Because Ambrose would have given it to me.

PHILIP. (*Slowly.*) Yes.

RACHEL. I understand and I'm very grateful. (*The bell goes again.*) We're keeping them waiting. (*She kisses him on the lips.*) Come! (*She takes his arm and pulls him with her towards the door.*)

FADE TO BLACKOUT

END OF ACT ONE

ACT TWO

Scene 1

The same. Philip's birthday. It is three months later. Kendall is pacing up and down. Seecombe stands by.

SEECOMBE. Seems hard to realise that Mr. Philip is twenty-five today. Seems only yesterday Mr. Ambrose brought him here—a mite not two years old.

KENDALL. Yes.

SEECOMBE. Pity the sunken garden's not finished for the occasion but the frosts were something cruel.

KENDALL. Yes.

SEECOMBE. Miss Louise is well, I hope, sir.

KENDALL. Yes.

SEECOMBE. I was saying to the mistress only the other day that we hadn't seen her since Christmas.

KENDALL. Yes.

SEECOMBE. (*Giving up.*) Well, if there's nothing you're wanting . . .

KENDALL. (*Rousing himself.*) Nothing, thank you, Seecombe.

SEECOMBE. Thank you, sir. I don't suppose Mr. Philip will be long. (*He goes out. Kendall continues pacing. Philip enters.*)

KENDALL. Where the devil have you been?

PHILIP. Swimming.

KENDALL. In this weather? You're mad.

PHILIP. The sea is clean. It's a kind of second baptism. I'm glad you've come.

KENDALL. You won't be when I've finished.

PHILIP. I suppose you're been to the bank?

KENDALL. Yes.

PHILIP. Well?

KENDALL. Why have you removed the Ashley collection? All of it.

PHILIP. That's my business. The jewels are my property now and I can do what I like with it.

42

KENDALL. What are you going to do?

PHILIP. That again is my business. You are no longer my trustee. I am of age.

KENDALL. Is Mrs. Ashley behind all this?

PHILIP. No.

KENDALL. I don't believe you.

PHILIP. As you wish.

KENDALL. Philip—what are you doing?

PHILIP. What should have been done long ago.

KENDALL. And what is that?

PHILIP. Rendering unto Caesar the things that are Caesar's.

KENDALL. I don't understand you.

PHILIP. You will. This morning I went to see Jeremy Trewin.

KENDALL. That lawyer in Bodmin?

PHILIP. Yes.

KENDALL. Why?

PHILIP. To draw up a Deed of Gift.

KENDALL. A Deed of Gift?

PHILIP. I am doing what Ambrose would have done if he had lived. I have given Barton, the house, all that it contains, and the estate, to my cousin Rachel for her lifetime.

KENDALL. Philip!

PHILIP. They are rightfully hers.

KENDALL. Dear God!

PHILIP. I have not told her yet. I intend to do so this evening.

KENDALL. You're insane.

PHILIP. I shall stay on at a salary and manage the estate for her.

KENDALL. Philip—you can't do this.

PHILIP. I've done it. It's all signed, sealed and witnessed. It's watertight, Uncle Nick. You can do nothing.

KENDALL. You fool. You besotted young fool. You're infatuated with the woman. A woman whose name is a by-word in Florence. (*Philip hits him. Kendall staggers and collapses onto a chair. Philip pours a drink and takes it to him.*)

PHILIP. Here. I'm sorry, Uncle Nick. But I won't have anyone saying a word against her. (*Kendall drinks.*)

KENDALL. (*Painfully.*) It is hers absolutely?

PHILIP. Unless she remarries.

KENDALL. I see. Can she sell any part of it?

PHILIP. No. Ambrose would have wished to keep the estate intact.

43

KENDALL. Philip—my dear boy—I implore you . . .

PHILIP. It's no good, Uncle Nick. This place belongs to my Cousin Rachel—to Ambrose's wife.

KENDALL. Have you ever thought of making her your wife?

PHILIP. Uncle Nick!

KENDALL. People are talking, Philip. She's been here nearly a year.

PHILIP. And who was eager for her to stay? You.

KENDALL. I was mistaken in her.

PHILIP. You *are* mistaken in her.

KENDALL. No, Philip, my eyes are open. Poor Ambrose. Poor Philip.

PHILIP. We can do without your pity.

KENDALL. Both of you absolutely ignorant of women. How could you be expected to withstand the wiles of one such as Mrs. Ashley?

PHILIP. You talk like someone in some vulgar novelette.

KENDALL. Philip—can't you *see*—can't you at least try to see? Are you so blind? She failed to get what she wanted from Ambrose—so she came here and got it from you.

PHILIP. She knows nothing about it—nothing.

KENDALL. She's been very clever. It's all been most carefully planned and you've fallen straight into her trap.

PHILIP. I have nothing more to say.

KENDALL. Well, I have. And after today I shall not be coming to Barton. And I will see that Louise follows my example. The Kendalls and the Ashleys have been friends for many generations but all things have to end. I will not return to your house—Ambrose's house—her house, now that you are sexually infatuated and like an impetuous young fool you've made it over to a scheming woman with a dubious background, who is ten years older than yourself. You have been swindled, Philip, my lad, and one day you will realise it. One day—and one day soon, she will have no further use for you, and you'll be homeless and penniless. Don't expect any sympathy from me, Philip—you won't get it. Everyone will laugh at you and say it serves you right.

PHILIP. Have you finished?

KENDALL. Yes.

PHILIP. Good. (*Louise enters.*)

LOUISE. Happy birthday, Philip.

PHILIP. Thank you.

44

LOUISE. I thought you might be here, Father. Philip, we'll bring your present tomorrow—I rode over so I couldn't carry it.

KENDALL. I'm afraid we won't be coming over tomorrow, Louise.

LOUISE. Why ever not? We haven't been here for ages. Have you two been quarreling?

PHILIP. No.

KENDALL. Yes.

LOUISE. Well, stop it, then. It's Philip's birthday. No one should quarrel on their birthday.

PHILIP. Thank you, Louise.

LOUISE. We'll look in after dinner tomorrow, Philip. Just for a few minutes. Come along, Father. (*Kendall stalks out of the room.*) Don't worry, Phil. I'll make him come.

PHILIP. It will be for the last time, Louise.

LOUISE. Why?

PHILIP. Ask him.

LOUISE. I'll ask him after tomorrow. We'll pretend that tomorrow is still your birthday. You look very angry, Philip.

PHILIP. I am very angry, Louise.

LOUISE. I must go, it's getting late.

PHILIP. Yes.

LOUISE. Till tomorrow.

PHILIP. I notice you don't ask after my Cousin Rachel.

LOUISE. No. Should I? (*She goes out. There is a pause, then Rachel comes out of her room and down the stairs.*)

RACHEL. I thought I heard voices.

PHILIP. The Kendalls.

RACHEL. Why didn't you let me know, it's so long since we saw them.

PHILIP. They were only here very briefly.

RACHEL. I am not as popular as I was. I wonder what could have set them against me. (*She seats herself on the sofa.*)

PHILIP. Uncle Nick's an old fool.

RACHEL. No, he isn't. Strange though—he liked me very well—he even flirted with me a little bit—at Christmas—perhaps he thought I had designs on him. Did they bring you a present?

PHILIP. They're bringing it tomorrow.

RACHEL. Ah, then I will ask him what I have done to offend him.

PHILIP. You have done nothing. It is me he is angry with.

RACHEL. Angry with you? Why?

45

PHILIP. Let's not talk about him. It's my birthday.

RACHEL. We should have had a party.

PHILIP. I'd rather be alone with you.

RACHEL. You should be surrounded by people of your own age, Philip, not dancing attendance on old women.

PHILIP. You're not old. You never will be old.

RACHEL. I found a grey hair this morning. Look.

PHILIP. I can't see it.

RACHEL. Look carefully. (*They are very close. Seecombe enters and they pull apart. Seecombe carries a tray with three glasses and a bottle of champagne.*)

SEECOMBE. The champagne, sir.

PHILIP. Thank you, Seecombe.

SEECOMBE. We will be drinking your health in the hall, sir.

PHILIP. Thank you. But you must have a glass with us, too, mustn't he, Rachel?

RACHEL. Of course. Where would Mr. Philip be without you, Seecombe?

SEECOMBE. Very good of you, I'm sure, Madam. (*He opens the champagne and pours three glasses.*) Your health, Mr. Philip.

RACHEL. Philip . . . (*They drink.*)

PHILIP. Thank you.

SEECOMBE. My old mother used to say "It's your birthday, may all your wishes come true . . ."

RACHEL. And did they?

SEECOMBE. She tried to make them come true if she could. We were very poor so I used not to wish for anything unusual.

RACHEL. Very wise, Seecombe. Have you wished, Philip?

PHILIP. Yes.

RACHEL. I hope you are as wise as Seecombe.

SEECOMBE. I have a small gift for you, Mr. Philip—a personal gift.

PHILIP. How kind of you, Seecombe, but—

SEECOMBE. (*Calling.*) James! (*James, who has evidently been expecting the call, enters carrying a picture. He gives it to Seecombe who hands it to Philip.*) Sir, this is only a trifle. A small memento of many years devoted service to the family. I hope you will not be offended and that I have not taken any liberty in assuming that you might be pleased to accept it as a gift.

PHILIP. This is very fine indeed. So fine in fact that I shall hang it in a place of honour.

SEECOMBE. Oh, sir. Do you consider, sir, that the likeness does me justice? Or has the arrtist given something of a harshness to the features? Especially the nose. I am not altogether satisfied.

PHILIP. Perfection in a portrait is impossible, Seecombe. This is as near to it as we shall get. Speaking for myself I could not be more delighted.

SEECOMBE. Then, Mr. Philip, that is all that matters.

PHILIP. Will you bring in the basket, Seecombe?

SEECOMBE. Very good, sir. (*He replaces his glass and goes out.*)

RACHEL. What's this?

PHILIP. A surprise.

RACHEL. A nice one?

PHILIP. I think you'll like it.

RACHEL. I love champagne. My first husband and I . . .

PHILIP. Yes?

RACHEL. He was very fond of it too. Poor Guido. Such a dreadful accident.

PHILIP. He died in an accident?

RACHEL. He had a young horse. Something frightened it and it bolted. My husband was flung against a wall. Thank God it was instantaneous.

PHILIP. Did you ever know any people called Dudley in Florence?

RACHEL. Not that I can remember. Why?

PHILIP. Oh, nothing. Louise said she had some friends there called Dudley.

RACHEL. No—I never met them. (*Seecombe enters carrying a large wicker hamper.*)

SEECOMBE. Where do you wnat this, sir. (*Philip indicates.*) Will that be all, Mr. Philip.

PHILIP. Yes, Goodnight, Seecombe.

SEECOMBE. Good night, sir. Good night, madam.

RACHEL. Good night. (*Seecombe goes out.*) Now let me guess.

PHILIP. You never will.

RACHEL. Something to eat?

PHILIP. No.

RACHEL. Something to drink?

PHILIP. No.

RACHEL. Something to wear?

PHILIP. I hope so. (*He takes a folded document out of his pocket.*) I want you to take this and read it in the morning.

47

RACHEL. (*Taking it.*) You're being very mysterious. (*She unfolds it.*)

PHILIP. No, not now. In the morning.

RACHEL. Very well. (*She puts the deed into a pocket. Philip pours out two more glasses.*) To you, again, dear Philip.

PHILIP. May my wishes come true.

RACHEL. May your wishes come true.

PHILIP. Amen.

RACHEL. I only hope they are wishes that your friends can help come true.

PHILIP. I have few friends.

RACHEL. I'm your friend, Philip. (*She puts out her hand and draws him down beside her. It is quite dark outside. They sit in a pool of light.*)

PHILIP. Every day you grow more and more beautiful.

RACHEL. That's the champagne talking.

PHILIP. It's true.

RACHEL. It must be the Cornish air. I shall be sorry to go, Philip.

PHILIP. You're not going.

RACHEL. But I must. Rainaldi wrote . . .

PHILIP. (*Interrupting.*) Don't let's speak of him tonight.

RACHEL. Very well.

PHILIP. How soft your hand is and so small. I believe I could hide both your hands in one of mine.

RACHEL. Something to wear, you said. A gown?

PHILIP. No.

RACHEL. And the surprise is for me?

PHILIP. Yes.

RACHEL. It should be for you, it's your birthday. (*He pours wine and hands her a glass. Rachel, dreamily.*) Look at the bubbles.

PHILIP. What did you do on your twenty-fifth birthday?

RACHEL. I forget. It's so long ago.

PHILIP. Ten years.

RACHEL. A lifetime. You were still a schoolboy. Did you like it at Harrow?

PHILIP. I always used to hate leaving Barton but when I got there—yes, I suppose I liked it.

RACHEL. I never went to school. My mother gave me lessons. Your hair wants cutting, Philip.

PHILIP. I know.

RACHEL. Why—it's wet.

PHILIP. I've been swimming.

RACHEL. You must be mad—in this weather?

PHILIP. That's what Uncle Nick said.

RACHEL. I wonder what put him against me . . .

PHILIP. Nobody.

RACHEL. Oh yes, somebody.

PHILIP. It doesn't matter. He doesn't matter.

RACHEL. He's your guardian.

PHILIP. He was. Drink up your champagne.

RACHEL. I shall be foxed—as Ambrose used to say. (*They laugh—they are not drunk but relaxed and happy.*)

PHILIP. I wish this evening could go on for ever.

RACHEL. I wish you'd open the hamper.

PHILIP. Very well, then. Close your eyes. (*She does so, and he opens the hamper and takes out the pearl collar which he clasps round her neck.*)

RACHEL. Philip—what are . . . ?

PHILIP. Open them. (*She opens her eyes and her fingers go to her neck.*)

RACHEL. Philip—the pearl collar!

PHILIP. Yes! No one can take it away from you now. (*She jumps to her feet and rushes to a mirror.*)

RACHEL. My collar! My lovely, lovely collar! (*Philip joins her. She puts her arms round him and they embrace. Rachel, muffled.*) I said I didn't mind. I did, Philip, I did. When I took it off I felt naked.

PHILIP. Damn him!

RACHEL. They're like silk against my skin. (*She draws away from him.*)

PHILIP. Come back to the sofa. (*He pulls her with him.*) Close your eyes.

RACHEL. Again?

PHILIP. Again. (*She does so. Excitedly he delves into the hamper and brings out handfuls of jewels which he showers on her. She opens her eyes.*)

RACHEL. Philip!

PHILIP. Do you like sapphires? They're yours. And emeralds . . . look at these rubies—and the diamonds . . . here's a bracelet . . . here's another . . . this was my grandmother's necklace . . . more sapphires . . . this tiara is all emeralds. This ring is supposed to have belonged to Mary Stuart and this one to Nelly Gwynn . . .

RACHEL. Philip, I'm dreaming . . .

PHILIP. They're all yours—and I'm all yours, dearest, dearest Rachel.

RACHEL. Philip . . . (*He buries his face in her lap.*)

PHILIP. I love you . . . I love you.

RACHEL. Hush . . . (*He lifts his face.*)

PHILIP. It's true.

RACHEL. You know me so little.

PHILIP. I know you are the most wonderful, most beautiful woman in the world.

RACHEL. Dear Philip. Sweet Philip.

PHILIP. My wish—make my wish come true.

RACHEL. But—Philip—

PHILIP. The only wish I could have, will ever have . . . you know what it is—you can't not know . . .

RACHEL. (*Slowly.*) Yes, I think I know.

PHILIP. Rachel.

RACHEL. Philip, are you sure?

PHILIP. Sure? It's the only thing I'm sure of in this world.

RACHEL. I'll be your first . . . ?

PHILIP. And only. Rachel, I'm so in love, I'm drowning. Help me.

RACHEL. My dear . . . (*She rises, scattering jewels and holds out her hand. He scrambles to his feet.*) Turn out the lamp. (*She picks up a candle and starts up the stairs. He turns out the lamp. At the top of the stairs she stops an looks down at him, then she goes into her room, leaving the door open. The candle flickers. Philip stumbles up the stairs and goes into her room. The door closes.*)

FADE OUT

FADE UP

ACT TWO

Scene 2

The same. It is afternoon, the following day.
Seecombe is pottering and Philip enters.

PHILIP. Mrs. Ashley back?

SEECOMBE. No, sir.

PHILIP. I don't understand it. She didn't tell me—er—last night that she was going into Bodmin.

SEECOMBE. She ordered the carriage early this morning, Mr. Philip, when you were out seeing the men.

PHILIP. Thank you, Seecombe.

SEECOMBE. They're taking their time with that bridge over the sunken garden, aren't they, sir?

PHILIP. Rome wasn't built in a day, Seecombe.

SEECOMBE. No, sir.

PHILIP. Mr. Kendall and Miss Louise may be looking in, Miss Louise told me she had a birthday present for me.

SEECOMBE. Shall I bring in the sherry, sir?

PHILIP. No, champagne . . . I'll ring.

SEECOMBE. Very good, sir. The champagne last night was to your liking?

PHILIP. It was excellent. (*Seecombe goes. Philip crosses and pours a generous brandy, drinks it and pours another, which he swallows quickly. Sound of a carriage Offstage. Philip hurries off. Sound of Louise's voice. Philip, looking glum, re-enters with Louise who is chattering brightly, and Kendall who looks grim. Louise carries a parcel which is obviously a gun.*)

LOUISE. I knew you wanted one of the new guns, so I sent to London for it. It only arrived yesterday—and here it is. With all our best wishes. (*She hands it to him.*)

PHILIP. Thank you, Louise, it is very kind of you. (*He rings.*)

LOUISE. Fancy you ringing. You always used to shout.

PHILIP. I ring when I remember.

LOUISE. How is the garden progressing?

PHILIP. Slowly. All this frost—and some of my best men laid up—one broke his leg and another down with a fever.

LOUISE. You be careful . . . there's a lot of fever about—and you're not looking as well as usual, is he, Father? (*Kendall shrugs, but does not answer. To cover the awkwardness, Louise rattles on.*) We saw Mary Pascoe in the village. I declare she's fatter than ever. Father said she looked like a stuffed armchair. Wasn't it naughty of him? Aren't you going to unwrap your gun, Philip?

PHILIP. Of course. (*He does so. Seecombe enters with champagne.*)

LOUISE. Good evening, Seecombe.

SEECOMBE. Good evening, Miss Louise, good evening sir. (*Kendall nods.*)

LOUISE. Oh, champagne! How lovely. We'll drink your health, Philip. I expect all the staff drank his health yesterday, didn't they, Seecombe?

51

SEECOMBE. Yes, Miss Louise.

PHILIP. It's a beauty . . . thank you again.

LOUISE. Presents are so difficult, don't you agree? What else did you get . . . I know the tenants' gift—but what else . . . ?

PHILIP. My cousin Rachel gave me a beautiful watch.

LOUISE. How nice . . . but haven't you Ambrose's?

PHILIP. Yes.

LOUISE. Still, I suppose it's a good thing to have two in case one goes wrong. (*Seecombe hands round champagne.*) Oh, thank you, Seecombe.

PHILIP. I'll have some brandy, Seecombe.

LOUISE. If I were rich I'd have champagne every night. Your health, Philip. (*She lifts her glass and drinks.*) Oh, isn't it delicious. I could go on drinking it for ever. (*The sound of a carriage is heard Offstage.*)

PHILIP. Excuse me . . . (*He hurries off, his face alight.*)

LOUISE. It must be *her*.

KENDALL. Drink up, Louise, you forced me to come and I came. Now we are going.

LOUISE. But, Father . . .

KENDALL. Hurry up.

LOUISE. Oh, very well. Yes, I realise you're furious with Philip— I think he's crazy myself but it *was* his birthday and . . . (*She stops as Philip enters with Rachel. He is all eagerness but she is very composed.*)

RACHEL. (*To Philip.*) I had to go into Bodmin on business, Philip. I didn't think it necessary to consult you . . . ah, Louise . . . and Mr. Kendall . . . (*Kendall bows.*)

LOUISE. Oh, er . . . good afternoon.

PHILIP. Champagne, Rachel?

RACHEL. (*Coolly.*) Thank you, no.

PHILIP. Seecombe see that the carriage goes round to the stables immmediately. We shall not be needing it again. (*Seecombe exits. Rachel looks coolly at Kendall and Louise. Philip looks puzzled.*)

LOUISE. We brought Philip's present over—that's it.

RACHEL. How very nice—but hasn't he several already?

LOUISE. Yes. He's very fortunate. Several guns and two watches.

KENDALL. (*Abruptly.*) We must be going. Come on, Louise . . .

PHILIP. A moment, please. Let me re-fill your glasses.

KENDALL. No, thank you, Philip.

PHILIP. I insist. (*He fills their glasses—he is a little drunk.*) I have a very important toast. Since last night I have been the happiest of

52

men. I believe, Uncle Nick, all our differences will be forgotten when I tell you and Louise to drink to Rachel—who is to be my wife. (*A gasp from Louise.*)

RACHEL. Have you quite lost your senses, Philip?

PHILIP. I am sorry it is premature, dearest, but—they are my oldest friends.

RACHEL. I think his birthday and the drink have gone to Philip's head. I apologise for this schoolboy folly, Louise. I trust you will forget it.

PHILIP. What are you saying, Rachel. You gave me your promise. You gave me your promise last night.

RACHEL. I think you had better go to your room, Philip, before you do any more damage.

KENDALL. Come, Louise.

RACHEL. Mr. Kendall, I know for some reason you have ceased to approve of me—but I do assure you there is not a word of truth in what Philip is saying.

KENDALL. I'm glad to hear of it. After all there is no need for marriage, you've gained your objective without it, have you not? (*Kendall goes out with Louise, leaving the door open. Rachel turns on Philip in a fury.*)

RACHEL. I could kill you!

PHILIP. But, Rachel . . . last night, in your bedroom—we made love.

RACHEL. So?

PHILIP. You wouldn't have consented if we were not going to get married.

RACHEL. You fool! You stupid country-bred fool! I let you make love to me because you had given me the jewels and because I had had too much champagne—because I was fond of you—but marriage . . . my God! do you really think I'd marry a schoolboy?

PHILIP. I can't believe it's you saying these things . . . Rachel . . . I implore you . . .

RACHEL. You disgust me. (*Philip recoils.*)

PHILIP. I did not disgust you last night.

RACHEL. Last night never happened.

PHILIP. Ah, but it did . . . when I awoke this morning you were in my arms . . . (*She tries to go past him but he bars the way.*) Why did you go into Bodmin?

RACHEL. To see Mr. Trewin.

PHILIP. Was not the Deed of Gift perfectly clear?

RACHEL. I just wanted it verified.

PHILIP. You haven't even thanked me.

RACHEL. I'd planned many things—things that would ensure you didn't suffer from giving me what was morally mine—but now . . . let me pass.

PHILIP. No.

RACHEL. Let me pass, Philip, or I will ring for Seecombe.

PHILIP. You whore! (*She slaps his face. He staggers back, but does not allow her to pass.*)

RACHEL. Let me pass.

PHILIP. Oh, Rachel, Rachel my love, say it's all a bad dream. Say you're going to be my wife. I love you. I love you . . .

RACHEL. Out of my way. (*Sound of a carriage offstage.*) Who's that?

PHILIP. I neither know nor care. Say you'll keep your promise, Rachel. (*She tries to pass him, but he holds her arm. The door bell rings.*)

RACHEL. Let me go!

PHILIP. (*Quietly.*) I'll never let you go, Rachel. Never. Do you understand? You're mine. After last night you're mine for ever. It is no use you're trying to run away because wherever you go I will follow you. You can go to the ends of the earth and I'll be there waiting for you. (*The bell rings again.*) You can never escape me. We are one person now and who can escape from himself? When you see your shadow you will see mine beside it. When you walk down a street, you will hear my footsteps following yours.

RACHEL. Philip don't . . . you're frightening me.

PHILIP. You would do well to be frightened, Rachel. You've never known love such as mine. It will be with you all your life— and mine and after your death . . . (*Rainaldi, a dark good looking man in his forties wearing a cloak and carrying a valise, enters through the open doorway. Rachel gives a little cry, frees herself and runs forward.*)

RACHEL. Rainaldi! My dear, dear Rainaldi . . . (*He takes both her hands and kisses them.*)

RAINALDI. Dear Rachel . . . Mr. Ashley?

PHILIP. (*Shortly.*) Yes.

RACHEL. I am so glad to see you. I did not expect you till next week.

RAINALDI. My business in London was over sooner than I thought.

RACHEL. Oh, it is so good to see you. Where are you staying?

RAINALDI. I have engaged a room at the "Rose & Crown."

RACHEL. For tonight only. Tomorrow you will come here.

RAINALDI. But—perhaps Signor Ashley—

RACHEL. (*Interrupting.*) I insist. Philip, give Signor Rainaldi a glass of wine. (*Dazedly Philip pours a drink.*) How is my lovely Florence?

RAINALDI. Very beautiful. The spring flowers are all out. The laburnums in the sunken garden are in their full glory.

RACHEL. I long to see them. I am making a sunken garden here, too. I will show you tomorrow. (*Philip hands Rainaldi a glass of wine.*)

RAINALDI. Thank you, Mr. Ashley. You are surprised to see me?

PHILIP. Yes.

RAINALDI. Rachel did not tell you I was in England.

PHILIP. No.

RAINALDI. I have been here three weeks. It was very cold in London.

RACHEL. You will find it warmer in Cornwall. How are all our friends?

RAINALDI. The Paolis gave their usual Spring Ball. It was magnificent. All Florence was there including your old admirer the Conte Firenze.

RACHEL. My dear Roberto . . . how is he?

RAINALDI. As handsome as ever. Isabella was there. They say she poisoned her husband—arsenic in the tisane. (*They both laugh.*)

RACHEL. And Paolo di Maggio. How is Paolo?

RAINALDI. It is rumoured that he will marry the youngest Mafiola girl.

RACHEL. No!

RAINALDI. Why not? She is young, pretty and what is more important extremely rich.

PHILIP. Excuse me . . . (*He goes out.*)

RAINALDI. He is not pleased. Why did you not tell him I was in England?

RACHEL. I was going to . . . why didn't you tell me you were coming today?

RAINALDI. Are you not happy to see me?

RACHEL. I'm thankful, Rainaldi. I can't tell you how thankful.

RAINALDI. Is something wrong?

RACHEL. Read this. (*She produces the Deed of Gift from her reticule and hands it to him.*)

RAINALDI. What is it?

RACHEL. Read it. (*He does so.*)

RAINALDI. Rachel!

RACHEL. It's all mine. Everything.

RAINALDI. How did you . . . ?

RACHEL. He's in love with me—the poor child. (*Pause—Rachel smiles triumphantly.*)

RAINALDI. (*Heavily.*) Yes, the poor child.

RACHEL. Is it not wonderful? All our troubles are over.

RAINALDI. Yes.

RACHEL. Why are you not pleased?

RAINALDI. I cannot help being sorry for anyone who loves you, Rachel.

RACHEL. He'll recover. He's young.

RAINALDI. There are some illnesses for which one does not recover. You are one of them.

RACHEL. My dear Rainaldi.

RAINALDI. I should know. I have had the Rachel sickness for many years. Sometimes I think I have recovered but when I see you again I know I have not. You are under my skin, Rachel, and there is no hope for me.

RACHEL. I have never heard you talk like this before.

RAINALDI. Nor will you again. Well—my dear, what are your plans?

RACHEL. I would like to leave here soon. I'm afraid all is not well between me and my cousin.

RAINALDI. But he has given you everything.

RACHEL. Yes, but he—he imagines that I had promised to marry him.

RAINALDI. And had you?

RACHEL. Never.

RAINALDI. You sometimes give the impression, my dear, of promising things—things you have no intention of giving.

RACHEL. Just because I was kind to him.

RAINALDI. Ah . . .

RACHEL. I am fond of him, Rainaldi, or was. Just now he frightened me.

RAINALDI. Young men take their disappointments too hard . . . now, if you will accept my advice . . .

RACHEL. I always do.

RAINALDI. Well—I advise you to get on good terms with him

56

again. It would look strange if you were not friends after his great generosity. He might make trouble.

RACHEL. How?

RAINALDI. I am not sure that this is absolutely watertight. (*He taps the Deed of Gift.*)

RACHEL. His lawyer says it is.

RAINALDI. I would prefer an expert opinion . . . till I get it, Rachel, well, you said you were fond of the boy.

RACHEL. I was.

RAINALDI. Be fond of him again. He seems a pleasant lad—and remarkably like Ambrose.

RACHEL. Yes . . .

RAINALDI. I must be going. The post chaise is waiting.

RACHEL. I'll send the carriage round tomorrow—about eleven.

RAINALDI. Are you sure it is wise?

RACHEL. Rainaldi—I need you.

RAINALDI. When you look at me like that I am unable to resist you. (*He kisses her hands.*) Until tomorrow. (*He goes to the door.*) Be fond of him again, Rachel. (*He goes out. Pause. Rachel rings the bell. Seecombe enters.*)

SEECOMBE. Yes, madam?

RACHEL. The tray, Seecombe, please. And tell Mr. Philip.

SEECOMBE. Very good, madam.

RACHEL. And Seecombe, we are having a visitor for a week or so. You can prepare the Blue Room—oh and see that the carriage goes to call for him at the Rose & Crown tomorrow at eleven.

SEECOMBE. I saw the post chaise madam as I was coming back from the stable. I hope I did not inconvenience you not being here to answer the bell.

RACHEL. That's all right, Seecombe. Our guest is an Italian friend of mine—a Signor Rainaldi. I will tell you about which food to order later.

SEECOMBE. Yes, madam. Foreign kickshaws I presume, madam?

RACHEL. Not at all, Seecombe—the roast beef of England. (*Seecombe, looking bewildered, goes. Rachel fidgets round the room. Philip enters.*)

PHILIP. You wanted me?

RACHEL. Yes. Philip, I'm sorry. Can we not be friends?

PHILIP. Friends?

RACHEL. Try to understand, my dear. I am deeply fond of you.

Surely I have proved that. My affection for you led you to expect—my dear, one day, I hope it will be soon—you will meet a girl of your own age and love her. What you imagine you feel for me will be like a dream—let it not be a bad dream, Philip.

PHILIP. It is you who do not understand, Rachel. I love you.

RACHEL. Philip, my dear—young men often imagine they love an older woman, but . . .

PHILIP. (*Interrupting.*) Why didn't you tell me Rainaldi was in England?

RACHEL. I was going to tell you.

PHILIP. Were you?

RACHEL. Of course. I suppose I forgot because it didn't seem very important. As to coming here—well, I was as surprised as you.

PHILIP. I am not too pleased that you invited him to stay here in my house.

RACHEL. My house, Philip dear.

PHILIP. Yes—your house.

RACHEL. Oh, Philip, my dear, it breaks my heart to have things so wrong between us. Let us be friends. Nothing matters except that we are friends.

PHILIP. Is that all we can be—friends?

RACHEL. For the moment—isn't that enough?

PHILIP. For the moment . . .

RACHEL. Who knows what may happen?

PHILIP. (*Eagerly.*) Rachel! (*Seecombe enters with the tray.*)

SEECOMBE. Your tisane, madame, and these came for you in the post, madam. (*He hands her a packet which she opens. Seecombe exits.*)

RACHEL. Ah—some more seeds for the garden . . . Coriander, Laburnum, Japonica . . .

PHILIP. What did you mean by—"for the moment"?

RACHEL. It is wise not to look too far ahead.

PHILIP. I meant what I said earlier. I will never leave you, Rachel.

RACHEL. Philip, that's absurd. You have your duties here. I have certain duties in Florence.

PHILIP. Then I will accompany you.

RACHEL. I shall probably be accompanied by Rainaldi.

PHILIP. That makes two of us.

RACHEL. Come to Florence, then, you will not like it.

PHILIP. I shall be with you.

RACHEL. I shall go on to Rome.

PHILIP. It doesn't matter where you go.

RACHEL. Philip—this is idiotic.

PHILIP. I have made up my mind, Rachel.

RACHEL. (*Slowly.*) Yes . . . yes I can see that you have.

PHILIP. How long will Rainaldi be here?

RACHEL. As long as—we have business to discuss.

PHILIP. I shall be interested.

RACHEL. Private business.

PHILIP. You can have nothing private from me any longer, Rachel. (*Pause. Rachel busies herself with the tisane tray.*) We could get married in Florence.

RACHEL. Philip—Philip are you ill? You're shivering.

PHILIP. And go to Rome for our honeymoon.

RACHEL. Philip—listen. Once and for all I am not going to marry y

PHILIP. Yes, you are. We were made for each other, Rachel.

RACHEL. You're mad!

PHILIP. I love you. (*She gives a shudder and hands him his cup.*) How wonderful to think that every day of our lives we shall be sitting somewhere, just the two of us, drinking our tisane . . . we shall grow older but it will be just the same—you will always be beautiful and I shall always adore you. We won't need other people because we shall have each other. You will send Rainaldi packing . . .

RACHEL. No.

PHILIP. Oh yes, my dear, (*He pulls a face.*) this tisane is more bitter than usual.

RACHEL. Philip—you *are* ill.

PHILIP. It is very warm . . . (*Rachel rings the bell.*) The summer will soon be here. You'll like Barton in the summer, Rachel. We'll go down to the sea . . . the sea . . . (*The cup falls from his hand.*) And we will go out into the meadows, and make love, and the sky will be so blue, so blue . . . (*He falls back in his chair as Seecombe enters.*)

RACHEL. Mr. Philip is ill, Seecombe. (*Seecombe goes to him.*)

SEECOMBE. Mr. Philip . . .

PHILIP. Just the two of us. Just the two of us . . . (*He collapses onto the floor.*)

FADE OUT

FADE UP
59

ACT TWO

SCENE 3

The same. A few days later.
Rainaldi is standing in front of the fireplace. Rachel comes downstairs.

RAINALDI. How is he?
RACHEL. He has a very high fever.
RAINALDI. What does the Doctor say?
RACHEL. He is worried. He is afraid it is affecting the brain.
RAINALDI. Like Ambrose.
RACHEL. Yes. Strange isn't it?
RAINALDI. Very strange.
RACHEL. Why are you looking at me like that?
RAINALDI. I was just thinking how unfortunate it was that you discovered that Ambrose had not signed the will until *after* he was dead.
RACHEL. What *do* you mean?
RAINALDI. We were so sure he had signed it. Oh well it doesn't matter now. All is well. You have all that he would have left you—and more—but it would be a pity if Philip were to die—like Ambrose.
RACHEL. Why should he? He is young and strong.
RAINALDI. Then we must hope that his youth and strength will pull him through—for his sake—and yours.
RACHEL. I don't understand you.
RAINALDI. I think you do.
RACHEL. (*Defensively.*) He went swimming and caught a chill.
RAINALDI. Yes?
RACHEL. It's the truth.
RAINALDI. I'm sure it is.
RACHEL. You sound as if you didn't believe me.
RAINALDI. I believe he went swimming and caught a cold.
RACHEL. What are you trying to say?
RAINALDI. What I have said. Nurse him very carefully, Rachel.
RACHEL. Why do I put up with you, Rainaldi?
RAINALDI. Habit, my dear. Or perhaps you cannot do without me.
RACHEL. I can do without you very well. I can do without any man!

60

RAINALDI. But you cannot do without the things that you gain through men. You use us like pawns in the chess game of your life. We are expendable. But take care you do not become reckless and make a false move.

RACHEL. I know what I am doing.

RAINALDI. Do you?

RACHEL. I am nursing a poor boy to whom I am devoted, making a sunken garden, and looking after my property. (*She says this lightly. Their eyes meet.*)

RAINALDI. I see.

RACHEL. I hope you do. It would be sad if we were to misunderstand each other after all these years.

RAINALDI. I shall never misunderstand you, Rachel. Love has not blinded me.

RACHEL. No?

RAINALDI. No. (*She smiles suddenly and holds out her hand. He kisses it.*) Rachel, why do you think I am here?

RACHEL. (*Pauses, suddenly laughs.*) You are my friend, Rainaldi.

RAINALDI. Your friend. How long is it since we first met?

RACHEL. I don't remember.

RAINALDI. I do. 16 years. At the Paolis . . . you were nineteen. You came into the ballroom wearing yellow taffetas, and the famous yellow diamonds of the Sangaletti . . . I was 24; and when I looked at you, it was as if the stars had come out in Heaven. (*Laughs.*) What did you think of me?

RACHEL. I thought you looked—interesting.

RAINALDI. Only interesting!

RACHEL. Very interesting.

RAINALDI. Perhaps if I had had money and a title. These things meant a great deal—to your mother. She was a woman of great appetite. She brought you up with a wrong sense of values, my poor Rachel . . . you were marred in the making. But what does it matter? You are Rachel. A creature of impulse; a creature of moods, of contradictions. You can be kind, you can be cruel; loveable-spiteful, sensual-puritanical. Unforgettable . . . You are Rachel. And I cannot do without you any more than you can do without me. And why? Because you lead a stormy life, my dear. A ship on a rough sea needs a steady helmsman. I am he. (*Louise enters hurriedly by the front door which is open.*)

LOUISE. Mrs. Ashley—they are saying in the village that Philip is very ill.

RACHEL. I'm afraid he is—Miss Kendall—Signor Rainaldi.

RAINALDI. Enchanted.

LOUISE. How do you do— (*To Rachel.*) What is the matter with him?

RACHEL. He went swimming—you remember—and caught a chill. Now he has a fever.

LOUISE. Can I see him?

RACHEL. I'm afraid not.

LOUISE. Why not?

RAINALDI. If you will excuse me . . . I have some business to attend to. (*He goes quickly.*)

LOUISE. Why not?

RACHEL. He is not well enough to see anyone at present.

LOUISE. *You* see him.

RACHEL. That is different.

LOUISE. Why is it different?

RACHEL. Miss Kendall, I know you are an old friend of Philip's . . . but . . .

LOUISE. Oh, why did you ever come here?

RACHEL. I beg your pardon.

LOUISE. You have bewitched him. He's not the Philip I knew . . . you *must* have promised to marry him.

RACHEL. I assure you I did not.

LOUISE. Then why did he say you were going to be his wife?

RACHEL. He was not himself.

LOUISE. Why?

RACHEL. Miss Kendall, this is a profitless discussion.

LOUISE. He has not been himself ever since he met you. Before you came he hated you for what you had done to Ambrose.

RACHEL. I think you had better go before you say anything you will regret.

LOUISE. You're an evil woman. You are notorious in Florence and you come here as mild as milk and bewitch a simple boy. You get him to give you all he possesses, and now that he is ill, I suppose you'll leave him, having squeezed him dry.

RACHEL. I shall ring for Seecombe to show you out.

LOUISE. I am not going without seeing Philip.

RACHEL. You are not seeing him.

LOUISE. What right have you to prevent me?

RACHEL. Every right. This is my house.

LOUISE. You may own the house, but you don't own Philip. (*Pause.*)

RACHEL. Miss Kendall, be reasonable. Philip is ill. Too ill to see

62

anyone. He has a bad fever. The doctor fears it may affect his brain.

LOUISE. As it did Ambrose. Strange that Philip should suffer in the same way as his cousin.

RACHEL. I am ringing for Seecombe. (*Louise bars her way to the bell.*)

LOUISE. That would be foolish. If it were known locally, and I would make sure it was known—ordering me out of the house of my oldest friend would not add to your popularity.

RACHEL. My popularity as you call it is a matter of supreme indifference to me.

LOUISE. I think not. You have done everything to court it. Visited the tenants, given them presents, flattered the County, charmed the Vicar. But perhaps now that you have everything, you will give up bothering.

RACHEL. If you will not go—then I will leave you.

LOUISE. I am seeing Philip.

RACHEL. No, Miss Kendall.

LOUISE. I will see him.

RACHEL. Have you no pride, no modesty? A young girl chasing a young man the way you chase Philip is most unseemly. If you were my daughter I would be ashamed of you.

LOUISE. Thank God I am not your daughter, for I would be ashamed of *you*. (*Rachel starts to speak but is interrupted by the sudden appearance of Philip at the top of the stairs. He looks very ill and wild.*)

RACHEL. Philip! Go back to bed at once!

PHILIP. Rachel . . . where have you been? (*He starts to stumble down the stairs.*)

RACHEL. Philip, my dear, go back to bed. You are ill.

PHILIP. I was asleep and you were not there.

RACHEL. I'll take you back and stay with you. Come . . .

LOUISE. Philip!

PHILIP. She wasn't there, Louise. My wife wasn't there.

RACHEL. Come.

PHILIP. I'm so thirsty.

RACHEL. I'll make you some tisane.

PHILIP. It's so bitter. Why is it so bitter, Rachel?

RACHEL. (*To Louise.*) Ring for Seecombe. (*Louise does so, she is shattered.*) Seecombe will bring you some lemonade.

PHILIP. A wife should stay with her husband. Why did you not stay with me, Rachel?

RACHEL. I'll stay with you, Philip. I'll stay with you.

PHILIP. You were sitting beside me. The sun was on your hair.

RACHEL. Let us go upstairs. I promise I'll sit beside you . . .

PHILIP. The sun was on your hair . . . (*Seecombe enters.*)

SEECOMBE. Mr. Philip!

RACHEL. Help me get him back to bed, Seecombe.

SEECOMBE. Yes, madam. (*He goes to Philip and between them they help him up the stairs. Louise stands rigid. They disappear and Louise sinks down onto the sofa and buries her face in her hands. She begins to cry. Rainaldi enters in travelling cloak, carrying a valise. She looks up.*)

RAINALDI. Miss Kendall—you are unwell.

LOUISE. No, no I am all right, thank you.

RAINALDI. Is there anything I can do?

LOUISE. No, there is nothing anyone can do. (*She rises.*) Goodbye, Signor. (*She goes out. He looks after her, puzzled. Seecombe comes down the stairs.*)

RAINALDI. Oh, Seecombe . . .

SEECOMBE. Yes, sir.

RAINALDI. I presume that Mrs. Ashley is looking after her patient.

SEECOMBE. Yes, sir.

RAINALDI. Give her this, will you. (*He hands him a note and picks up his valise.*)

SEECOMBE. You're not leaving, sir?

RAINALDI. I'm afraid so. Guests are not welcome in a house where there is sickness.

SEECOMBE. I will order the carriage to be sent round.

RAINALDI. No need. It is but a step to the village and I can get a post-chaise. (*He hands Seecombe some money.*)

SEECOMBE. Thank you, sir.

RAINALDI. Thank you for looking after me so well. (*He nods at Seecombe and goes off. Rachel appears at the head of the stairs.*)

RACHEL. Mr. Philip would like some lemonade, Seecombe.

SEECOMBE. Very good, madam. The Signor left this note for you.

RACHEL. What do you mean?

SEECOMBE. He's gone, madam, and left you this note.

RACHEL. Gone?

SEECOMBE. Yes, madam. (*She comes down the stairs and takes the note.*) I'll fetch the lemonade, madam. (*He goes off. She tears open the note and reads it. She looks puzzled, reads it again then crumples it up as Seecombe re-enters with a jug on a tray.*)

RACHEL. Seecombe, I shall want the carriage tomorrow afternoon.

SEECOMBE. Very good, madam.

RACHEL. Miss Kendall?

SEECOMBE. She must have gone while we were with Mr. Philip, madam.

RACHEL. Yes. Thank you, Seecombe . . . I'll take that. (*She takes the jug from him.*) I shall be sitting with Mr. Philip. See that we are not disturbed.

SEECOMBE. Very good, madam. (*She goes upstairs. He stands looking after her.*)

FADE DOWN

FADE UP

ACT TWO

SCENE 4

The same. Three weeks later. Afternoon.
Philip, better but shaky and in a dressing gown is being helped down the stairs by James. Seecombe enters.

SEECOMBE. That's right . . . slowly does it. Over to the fire, Mr. Philip. You must keep warm. (*James steers Philip to a chair by the fire.*) It's good to see you up again, sir.

PHILIP. How long has it been, Seecombe?

SEECOMBE. A good three weeks, sir. You had us very worried, sir, you as had never been ill in your life . . . that'll do, boy. (*James goes off.*)

PHILIP. Where's the mistress?

SEECOMBE. Gone shopping, sir. She goes regular like most afternoons, buying new curtains and such like . . . "Seecombe" she says to me "Seecombe, you won't know the place when I've finished with it . . ." By the way, sir, you remember those clothes of Mr. Ambrose's you gave me to give to the tenants?

PHILIP. Of course. I hope they were appreciated.

SEECOMBE. Oh yes, indeed, sir. I took the liberty of keeping his jacket for myself, sir.

65

PHILIP. I'm glad—Mr. Ambrose would have been glad too.

SEECOMBE. I wore it for the first time yesterday and I found this in the pocket. It's addressed to you, sir. (*He hands him a letter.*)

PHILIP. From Mr. Ambrose.

SEECOMBE. Looks like he didn't have time to post it.

PHILIP. Yes . . . thank you, Seecombe.

SEECOMBE. Can I get you anything, sir?

PHILIP. What—oh, yes, a hot brandy and water.

SEECOMBE. Very good, sir. (*He goes out and Philip opens the letter.*)

PHILIP. (*Reading slowly.*) "Philip—They are plotting something—Rachel and Rainaldi . . . when I approach they fall silent. They want me out of the way. Can they be plotting to murder me? Come quickly for God's sake." (*James comes in with the hot brandy and water. He puts it down by Philip, then makes a grimace of pain and puts his hand to his ear. Philip, dully.*) What's the matter?

JAMES. It's the ear-ache, Mr. Philip. I've got it cruel. 'Tis all that waiting on the quayside every afternoon for the mistress. It was that bad William took my place today.

PHILIP. The quayside? There are no shops on the quayside.

JAMES. No, sir, but the mistress goes to the Rose & Crown to see the foreign gentleman.

PHILIP. The foreign gentleman?

JAMES. The one what was staying here. Will that be all, sir?

PHILIP. Yes, that will be all. (*James goes. Philip takes out the letter and reads it again. The sound of a carriage Offstage. He puts the letter away and takes a sip of brandy. Rachel enters.*)

RACHEL. Philip! My dear how good to see you up again!

PHILIP. You've been shopping.

RACHEL. Oh, Philip—should you be drinking brandy? Let me make you a tisane.

PHILIP. No thank you. What did you buy?

RACHEL. Oh, this and that . . . hangings for the Blue Room.

PHILIP. I'd like to see them.

RACHEL. So you shall.

PHILIP. Where are they?

RACHEL. They're sending them by carrier. How are you feeling, Philip?

PHILIP. A bit weak. What else did you buy?

RACHEL. I really can't remember. Are you warm enough, my dear? It's nearly May—but very chilly out.

PHILIP. Yes, it must be cold by the sea. There's always a wind on the quayside.

RACHEL. I must go and take off my things. Shall we have an early dinner?

PHILIP. Why not?

RACHEL. I've ordered your favorite—boiled chicken with bacon and parsley sauce.

PHILIP. Which you never had in Italy.

RACHEL. No—we cook chicken in many different ways but not with bacon and parsley sauce. Personally, I find it delicious.

PHILIP. I'm glad. I wonder if your friend Signor Rainaldi would agree . . . how long ago did he leave us—I forget.

RACHEL. Several weeks now he felt that guests should not intrude when there is sickness in the house.

PHILIP. How wise, so he went to the Rose & Crown instead. (*Their eyes lock. There is a pause.*)

RACHEL. (*Steadily.*) Yes, he went to the Rose & Crown instead.

PHILIP. And you visit him every afternoon.

RACHEL. We have business to discuss.

PHILIP. Why did you lie to me—saying you were shopping?

RACHEL. Because I know you hate Rainaldi.

PHILIP. Yes, I hate him.

RACHEL. He is the only true friend I have in the world. He knows me for what I am and it makes no difference.

PHILIP. And what are you?

RACHEL. A woman. A woman like all others. A creature of impulse. Someone with all the human weaknesses. Good and bad mixed together. A woman who has known great sorrow.

PHILIP. Such as?

RACHEL. I loved Ambrose. He died. (*Philip hands her a letter.*) What's this?

PHILIP. Read it. (*She does so.*)

RACHEL. My poor Ambrose. My poor, poor Ambrose.

PHILIP. Is Rainaldi your lover?

RACHEL. How dare you!

PHILIP. Why did you not marry him when Ambrose died. Ah, but I was forgetting—you had not got the money then.

RACHEL. Philip!

PHILIP. What a fool I've been. How you must have laughed at me.

RACHEL. No, Philip, no.

PHILIP. (*Taking back the letter and reading.*) "Are they plotting to murder me?"

RACHEL. He was out of his mind.

PHILIP. I wonder.

RACHEL. You are out of your mind, too, to take any notice of such a letter.

PHILIP. I *was* out of my mind.

RACHEL. Philip, you are still not well. You don't know what you are saying.

PHILIP. Ah, but I do, Rachel. I am saying that Rainaldi is your lover and that Ambrose died very conveniently.

RACHEL. I am leaving this house tomorrow, or you are.

PHILIP. Where do you suggest I go?

RACHEL. Wherever you wish.

PHILIP. Florence? I would like a word with Ambrose's doctor.

RACHEL. Why?

PHILIP. His collapse was very sudden, was it not? (*Seecombe enters with the tisane tray.*)

RACHEL. Thank you, Seecombe.

PHILIP. I'll have another hot toddy, Seecombe.

SEECOMBE. Very good, sir. (*He goes out.*)

PHILIP. Hot brandy may not be good for me but at least it's safe.

RACHEL. I am beginning to understand.

PHILIP. Good.

RACHEL. You believe the letter—you think Ambrose did not die naturally.

PHILIP. I only know what he said in this letter—and the other letters.

RACHEL. The other letters?

PHILIP. Why do you think I went to Florence?

RACHEL. Because Ambrose was ill.

PHILIP. Because Ambrose was ill—and frightened. Because of what he had written about you.

RACHEL. What did he say?

PHILIP. He said money was the only way to your heart. He said you lied. I know you lie. He said: "She has done for me, Rachel my torment . . ."

RACHEL. (*In a whisper.*) He said that . . .

PHILIP. He begged me to come quickly. I came. I found he had died suddenly and was buried just as suddenly—and now I find that (*He taps the letter.*) Rainaldi is at the Rose & Crown. I have also had a fever—an unaccountable fever. I find it—strange.

RACHEL. Are you accusing me of murdering Ambrose?

PHILIP. I said I found it—strange.

RACHEL. I am trying to keep calm, Philip. I find it difficult. I am saying to myself—he is still a sick man. But however sick you are—what you are saying is monstrous. So monstrous it is almost laughable—if I could laugh. You are accusing me and my dear Rainaldi of—of murdering Ambrose. Why? Why? I had nothing to gain by his death. He left nothing to me . . . I had everything to lose. A husband, a home, everything. Your insane jealously of Rainaldi has upset the balance of your mind, Philip. What you are saying to me is actionable—if I wished to take action. But I have been fond of you—very fond and very grateful and now that you are better, I am returning to Florence.

PHILIP. When?

RACHEL. The day after tomorrow.

PHILIP. Don't go!

RACHEL. After such an accusation, how can I stay?

PHILIP. I don't care what you have done. I love you.

RACHEL. Oh, Philip . . .

PHILIP. I love you with every bit of my being. I *cannot* lose you. I know you lie. I know that money is your God. I know you plotted with Rainaldi—but it doesn't matter. You are my life, Rachel. Without you I am nothing. Without you I cannot go on living. Say my suspicions have been a bad dream. You loved me once . . . say you love me still.

RACHEL. I loved you? I never loved you. Not for an instant.

PHILIP. Not . . . for . . . an . . . instant . . . ?

RACHEL. A green boy like you? I have known men. (*Seecombe enters with the hot toddy.*)

SEECOMBE. Here you are, sir.

RACHEL. Seecombe, I shall be leaving for Italy the day after tomorrow.

SEECOMBE. Oh madam—will you be gone long?

RACHEL. Some time, I think. I have a lot to do and many friends to see.

SEECOMBE. We shall miss you, madam, all of us.

RACHEL. I should like the carriage brought round about four o'clock. I shall spend the night in Bodmin.

SEECOMBE. Yes, madam. It's a pity you have to go before the sunken garden is quite finished.

RACHEL. When I return—perhaps next year—the bulbs will have had time to grow and the trees will be out.

SEECOMBE. Next year, madam. That's a long time—isn't it, Mr. Philip?

PHILIP. Yes.

SEECOMBE. As I said we will miss you, madam.

RACHEL. Thank you, Seecombe.

SEECOMBE. Have you finished with the tray, madam?

RACHEL. Yes, you may take it. (*Seecombe takes the tray and goes.*)

PHILIP. I suppose Rainaldi will be going with you.

RACHEL. Yes.

PHILIP. I expect, also, that you will want me to go on managing the estate while you are away.

RACHEL. Why not? What else can you do? You have no profession.

PHILIP. No.

RACHEL. Oh, Philip—why do you force me to be so cruel?

PHILIP. I force you?

RACHEL. Tear up Ambrose's letters. Give your jealousy and your absurd suspicions nothing to feed on. They do not harm me, Philip, they harm you.

PHILIP. I believe Ambrose. He would not have written such letters without cause.

RACHEL. You've kept them from me all these months.

PHILIP. Yes. The moment I saw you I loved you. I believed what you said about his illness changing him.

RACHEL. It's the truth.

PHILIP. You never had any pearls, your first husband was not killed in an accident, Rainaldi had gone back to Italy—you have lied to me so often, Rachel . . . why should you not lie about Ambrose's death?

RACHEL. You have not an atom of proof.

PHILIP. No.

RACHEL. If one word of your wild accusations got to Rainaldi's ears . . .

PHILIP. What then?

RACHEL. He is a lawyer. He would know what to do. (*She moves towards the stairs.*)

PHILIP. Where are you going?

RACHEL. To my room. To pack.

FADE DOWN

FADE UP
70

ACT TWO

SCENE 5

The same. Afternoon, two days later.
Philip is sitting in the armchair staring at nothing. Seecombe enters.

SEECOMBE. Excuse me, sir, I have a message from the foreman who's working on the ravine in the sunken garden.

PHILIP. Oh, yes?

SEECOMBE. It's about the bridge across it, sir.

PHILIP. Yes?

SEECOMBE. Well, he asked me to tell you it weren't safe to stand on, sir. The supports aren't in yet, so it won't take no weight—and the drop is twenty-five feet, sir . . .

PHILIP. Thank you, Seecombe, *I'll remember. (James appears at the head of the stairs, carrying a trunk.)*

SEECOMBE. Put that in the porch, James.

JAMES. Yes, Mr. Seecombe.

SEECOMBE. Is that the lot?

JAMES. One more to come. *(He goes off with the trunk.)*

SEECOMBE. Yes, we're going to miss Mrs. Ashley sir. *(Philip does not reply. Seecombe turns to go—then, remembering something, turns back.)* Oh, and Tamlyn says can he cut down the laburnum in he Long Walk—they're hanging over the wall into Lacy's Meadows where the cows are, and their seeds is poison.

PHILIP. Poison? Laburnum seeds?

SEECOMBE. Didn't you know that, Mr. Philip, and you a country boy? Deadly poison they are. The Tregassick boys ate them and all three of them died. I remember the funeral—from here to Bodmin and all the women crying.

PHILIP. Laburnum seeds . . . *(The bell rings.)*

SEECOMBE. Now who can that be? *(He goes to let in Louise and Kendall.)*

PHILIP. *(Rising.)* Louise! Uncle Nick!

KENDALL. Louise insisted on coming and she wouldn't come alone. Besides I wanted to see you—about business.

PHILIP. Yes?

KENDALL. Later.

LOUISE. It's wonderful to see you well and about again.

KENDALL. You've had a bad time by all accounts.

PHILIP. Yes . . . what can I offer you?

KENDALL. Nothing. I must see Tamlyn before he goes. I'll call back for Louise and we can talk then. (*James re-enters and goes upstairs.*)

PHILIP. Please have a drink before you go, Uncle Nick—to show there's no ill-feeling.

KENDALL. Very well. (*Philip crosses and pours wine.*)

LOUISE. You're thinner.

KENDALL. What exactly was the matter?

PHILIP. A fever. Dr. Mortimer was puzzled—he said it looked like Roman fever . . .

LOUISE. Roman fever—here in Cornwall . . .

PHILIP. Yes. (*Handing him a glass.*) Here you are, sir. Louise?

LOUISE. No, thank you.

KENDALL. We were all very worried, I don't mind telling you.

LOUISE. You ought to go away for a holiday.

PHILIP. I'm thinking of going abroad . . . it'll probably be a wild goose chase but there's someone I particularly want to see—a doctor.

LOUISE. A doctor? Then you still aren't well . . .

PHILIP. I'm not seeing him on account.

LOUISE. Oh? (*James comes downstairs with a trunk and goes out.*)

KENDALL. You're going away, Philip?

PHILIP. No. Mrs. Ashley is leaving this afternoon.

LOUISE. What!

PHILIP. Are you surprised?

LOUISE. Yes . . . yes, I suppose I am.

KENDALL. She is returning to Florence?

PHILIP. Yes.

KENDALL. Very wise of her. There has been much talk in the neighbourhood . . . (*He goes out.*)

LOUISE. Why is she going so suddenly? When I came to see you when you were ill, she said nothing about going.

PHILIP. Did you come to se me?

LOUISE. Yes—don't you remember?

PHILIP. No.

LOUISE. You came down and spoke to me.

PHILIP. I don't remember.

LOUISE. She said I wasn't to see you and I was angry, and then you came down looking for her.

PHILIP. You don't like her, do you?

LOUISE. No.

PHILIP. Why? (*James re-enters and goes upstairs.*)

LOUISE. Because of what she did to you and what she might have done to Ambrose. (*There is a pause.*) Phil—can I ask you something?

PHILIP. Of course.

LOUISE. You won't be angry?

PHILIP. No.

LOUISE. Promise?

PHILIP. Promise.

LOUISE. Did she ever say she loved you?

PHILIP. I—I took it for granted.

LOUISE. She was your mistress?

PHILIP. Louise!

LOUISE. You said you wouldn't be angry.

PHILIP. I regarded her as my wife.

LOUISE. It—it all happened before you had given her Barton?

PHILIP. Yes.

LOUISE. And afterwards?

PHILIP. There was no afterwards.

LOUISE. Oh, poor Philip! my dear, dear Philip . . .

PHILIP. Don't be sorry for me, Louise . . . (*There is a pause.*)

LOUISE. Philip—do you—do you believe what you believed about Ambrose—before she came here? (*Before he can reply—Rachel's voice is heard Offstage.*)

RACHEL. (*Offstage.*) That is all thank you, James.

JAMES. (*Offstage.*) Very good, madam. (*Rachel appears at the head of the stairs followed by James carrying a parcel.*)

RACHEL. Ah, Miss Kendall. (*She descends the stairs.*) How very pleasant. (*She goes to Louise and Philip, James goes off.*) Isn't it wonderful to see Philip well again? He's quite his old self, don't you think?

LOUISE. Yes.

RACHEL. You must look after him for me while I am away.

LOUISE. You are going for long?

RACHEL. Who can tell? Florence is so beautiful at this time of the year. And so gay. We go for picnics up in the hills and take musicians with us. They play while we eat and drink the Tuscan wine. You have not been to Italy, Miss Kendall?

LOUISE. No.

RACHEL. Ah—you should. Perhaps on your honeymoon. Italy is the only place for honeymoons.

LOUISE. Did you spend both yours there, Mrs. Ashley?

RACHEL. Dear Miss Kendall, how clever of you to guess. Now, Philip, I am going to have a last look at our sunken garden. The bridge over the ravine is up and the garden should be ready for planting quite soon. I have left instructions with the gardeners and they know precisely what to do. (*James comes in and crosses behind her and goes off.*) The foreman is a very intelligent man. I must employ him again. I have a fancy for a gazebo on the knoll above the lakes where the azaleas grow. I shall not be long. Will you be here when I return, Miss Kendall?

LOUISE. I may not be. Father is coming to collect me.

RACHEL. Give him my good wishes. It has been some time since he called on me. I shall not be long, Philip. What at beautiful afternoon . . . I almost wish . . .

PHILIP. Yes?

RACHEL. That I was not going. I have come to love Cornwall and I have a fancy that I shall leave part of me behind—among the wild seas and the grey rocks, and when I am sitting in the garden of the villa, drinking my tisane under the laburnums, I shall remember stormy skies and cobbled streets . . . but I shall have the sunshine—and without sunshine I cannot live. (*She smiles and turns to go.*)

PHILIP. (*Urgently.*) Have a care! (*She turns back.*)

RACHEL. Have a care?

PHILIP. (*Slowly.*) Do not walk too much in the sun.

RACHEL. (*Smiling.*) I always walk in the sun, Philip—did you not know that? (*She unfurls her parasol and goes out slowly. Louise looks at Philip. He is evidently in a terrible state of nervous tension.*)

LOUISE. Philip! What's the matter? Do you mind so terribly that she is going?

PHILIP. Louise—do you believe in justice?

LOUISE. Justice?

PHILIP. Do you believe in retribution?

LOUISE. I don't know what you're talking about.

PHILIP. When the law is powerless, has a man the right to take the law into his own hands?

LOUISE. I still don't know what you're talking about.

PHILIP. I loved Ambrose, Louise. He was the Father I had never known. We had wonderful times together. We would go riding across the fields down to the sea and watch the fishing boats. When the catch came in, we'd go down to the quay and buy pollock and bring it back and Seecombe would take them and tell cook how to make the special pollock pie with potatoes and cheese on the top. After dinner we would sit by the fire and talk. Ambrose would tell me what Barton was like when he was a boy and his mother was alive. How they gave great balls and all the countryside came in their finery. How his mother used to wear the pearl collar . . . the pearl collar . . .

LOUISE. Philip, you're ill.

PHILIP. (*Hysterically.*) Vengeance is mine, I will repay, said the Lord. But He doesn't, Louise. He doesn't.

LOUISE. Sit down and rest and I . . .

PHILIP. (*Interrupting.*) Rest? You tell me to rest? I don't think I'll ever rest again, Louise. You see, I'll never be really sure. I *must* be sure. I *am* sure.

LOUISE. Sure of what?

PHILIP. It all adds up, the letters, his death, the lies, the laburnum seeds, Rainaldi . . . yes, it all adds up. But there is no proof—there never will be any proof. I had to do it, Louise . . . I had to do it . . . (*Abruptly.*) remember "Hamlet" . . . ?

LOUISE. Hamlet? I read him at school but I don't see . . .

PHILIP. (*Interrupting.*) Hamlet had no proof either, or he would have acted sooner . . . what was that? Did you hear anything?

LOUISE. No.

PHILIP. Ambrose loved life. He was still a young man, Loiuse, in his forties. He'd looked forward to seeing the trees he had planted grow tall and strong. The larch planatation, Louise . . . he told me . . . "As your sons grow tall, so will the larches, Philip . . ." (*He sinks down and buries his face in his hands.*)

LOUISE. Philip . . .

PHILIP. I've been through Heaven and Hell . . . I am in Hell now, Rachel, my torment . . .

LOUISE. You've the fever again, Philip. Now please . . .

PHILIP. (*Interrupting.*) Ambrose took me once to the crossroads to see a man they had hanged for murdering his wife. They used to hang murderers at the crossroads you know. He was swinging there in the wind like a sack, his face shrunk like leather, his hands . . .

LOUISE. (*Interrupting.*) Stop Philip! It's horrible! Stop! (*Kendall re-enters. Philip has buried his face in his hands. Kendall looks at him and then turns to Louise.*)

KENDALL. Anything wrong?

LOUISE. Philip . . . he's . . . he's still not quite well.

KENDALL. Then I'll be brief. (*Louise makes a movement.*) If you'll just wait in the porch a moment, my dear. (*She goes out with a worried backward look at Philip.*) I've had a letter from Couch. (*Philip looks up.*) Are you sure you're all right? (*Philip nods.*) He says Mrs. Ashley has been to see him. She's given back the jewels.

PHILIP. (*Dully.*) She's what?

KENDALL. (*Patiently.*) Given back the jewels and revoked the Deed of Gift. She said she'd come to the conclusion that it was grossly unfair and that anyway she preferred to live in Italy. We've misjudged her Philip. (*Philip jumps to his feet—horrified.*) I am very much to blame. That friend of Louise's—I've learned that her Mother is well known for spreading scandal. What is it? Philip you're shaking!

PHILIP. Nothing . . . nothing.

KENDALL. Couch asked her why she had accepted everything in the first place, and she said she had taken them because it was so incredibly immature of you to give everything away to a woman you hardly knew, and she was afraid you were not a responsible person to leave in charge of Ambrose's beloved Barton. I've come to the conclusion that she really loved Ambrose, Philip.

PHILIP. Oh, my God! (*Suddenly there are a series of screams off stage.*)

KENDALL. Louise! (*He runs out.*)

PHILIP. (*Gabbling.*) I had to do it . . . I didn't know . . . I had to do it . . . oh, God, I didn't know . . . (*He sinks to his knees on the floor. Kendall re-enters, half carrying an hysterical Louise.*)

LOUISE. The bridge . . . she stood on it . . . she stood on it . . . she fell . . . Father, she fell . . . (*Kendall drops her into a chair.*)

KENDALL. Who fell?

LOUISE. Mrs. Ashley. (*Kendall stares at her for a second and then runs out.*) Philip . . . she fell . . . (*Philip, by now totally unhinged by what he has done, looks at her quite calmly.*)

PHILIP. (*Quietly.*) They used to hang murderers at the cross roads but not any more. There they used to swing in the wind—to and fro, to and fro, to and fro, to and fro, to and . . .

SLOW CURTAIN

END OF PLAY

76

PROPERTY PLOT

Furniture
Assorted tables, chairs, lamps etc. (Suitable for an English country manor)
Sofa
Fireplace
Cupboard, with wine, brandy, glasses
   Act One—Scene 1
Off Stage
Candle, in jam pot
Valise
Small traveling case
   Act One—Scene 2
Off Stage
Leather case
Small package, with amber necklace
Riding crop
Personal
Letters (2) (Philip)
   Act One—Scene 3
On Stage
Silver rose bowl, with flowers
Off Stage
Candle
Silver tray, with tea things (teapot, cups, hot water)
   Act One—Scene 4
On Stage
Shawl
Off Stage
Tray, with decanters of port and madeira
Silver dish, with biscuits
Large trunks (2) (one with books; one with clothing, including jacket and hat)
Tray, with tea things
   Act One—Scene 5
Off Stage
Legal document
Tray, with tea things
Silver salver, with letters
   Act One—Scene 6
On stage
Christmas tree, in tub

Off Stage
Parcels (2)
Apron
Personal
List and pile of cards (Seecombe)
Pearl collar (Philip)
Small box, with cufflinks (Rachel)
   Act Two—Scene 1
Off Stage
Tray, with bottle of champagne and glasses (3)
Portrait of Seecombe
Large wicker hamper, with jewelry, including pearl collar
Personal
Folded document, in pocket (Philip)
   Act Two—Scene 2
Off Stage
Parcel, with rifle
Bottle of champagne, on tray, with glasses
Valise
Tray, with tea things
Packets of seeds
Personal
Deed of Gift, in handbag (Rachel)
   Act Two—Scene 3
Off Stage
Valise
Tray, with pitcher of lemonade
Personal
Note and money (Rainaldi)
   Act Two—Scene 4
Off Stage
Glasses of hot brandy and water (2)
Tray, with tea things
Personal
Letter (Seecombe)
   Act Two—Scene 5
Off Stage
Trunks (2)
Parcel
Parasol

NEW PLAYS

★ **HONOUR by Joanna Murray-Smith.** In a series of intense confrontations, a wife, husband, lover and daughter negotiate the forces of passion, history, responsibility and honour. "HONOUR makes for surprisingly interesting viewing. Tight, crackling dialogue (usually played out in punchy verbal duels) captures characters unable to deal with emotions ... Murray-Smith effectively places her characters in situations that strip away pretense." –*Variety* "... the play's virtues are strong: a distinctive theatrical voice, passionate concerns ... HONOUR might just capture a few honors of its own." –*Time Out Magazine* [1M, 3W] ISBN: 0-8222-1683-3

★ **MR. PETERS' CONNECTIONS by Arthur Miller.** Mr. Miller describes the protagonist as existing in a dream-like state when the mind is "freed to roam from real memories to conjectures, from trivialities to tragic insights, from terror of death to glorying in one's being alive." With this memory play, the Tony Award and Pulitzer Prize-winner reaffirms his stature as the world's foremost dramatist. "... a cross between Joycean stream-of-consciousness and Strindberg's dream plays, sweetened with a dose of William Saroyan's philosophical whimsy ... CONNECTIONS is most intriguing ..." –*The NY Times* [5M, 3W] ISBN: 0-8222-1687-6

★ **THE WAITING ROOM by Lisa Loomer.** Three women from different centuries meet in a doctor's waiting room in this dark comedy about the timeless quest for beauty – and its cost. "... THE WAITING ROOM ... is a bold, risky melange of conflicting elements that is ... terrifically moving ... There's no resisting the fierce emotional pull of the play." –*The NY Times* "... one of the high points of this year's Off-Broadway season ... THE WAITING ROOM is well worth a visit." –*Back Stage* [7M, 4W, flexible casting] ISBN: 0-8222-1594-2

★ **THE OLD SETTLER by John Henry Redwood.** A sweet-natured comedy about two church-going sisters in 1943 Harlem and the handsome young man who rents a room in their apartment. "For all of its decent sentiments, THE OLD SETTLER avoids sentimentality. It has the authenticity and lack of pretense of an Early American sampler." –*The NY Times* "We've had some fine plays Off-Broadway this season, and this is one of the best." –*The NY Post* [1M, 3W] ISBN: 0-8-222-1642-6

★ **LAST TRAIN TO NIBROC by Arlene Hutton.** In 1940 two young strangers share a seat on a train bound east only to find their paths will cross again. "All aboard. LAST TRAIN TO NIBROC is a sweetly told little chamber romance." –*Show Business* "... [a] gently charming little play, reminiscent of Thornton Wilder in its look at rustic Americans who are to be treasured for their simplicity and directness ..." –*Associated Press* "The old formula of boy wins girls, boy loses girl, boy wins girl still works ... [a] well-made play that perfectly captures a slice of small-town-life-gone-by." –*Back Stage* [1M, 1W] ISBN: 0-8222-1753-8

★ **OVER THE RIVER AND THROUGH THE WOODS by Joe DiPietro.** Nick sees both sets of his grandparents every Sunday for dinner. This is routine until he has to tell them that he's been offered a dream job in Seattle. The news doesn't sit so well. "A hilarious family comedy that is even funnier than his long running musical revue *I Love You, You're Perfect, Now Change.*" –*Back Stage* "Loaded with laughs every step of the way." –*Star-Ledger* [3M, 3W] ISBN: 0-8222-1712-0

★ **SIDE MAN by Warren Leight.** 1999 Tony Award winner. This is the story of a broken family and the decline of jazz as popular entertainment. "... a tender, deeply personal memory play about the turmoil in the family of a jazz musician as his career crumbles at the dawn of the age of rock-and-roll ..." –*The NY Times* "[SIDE MAN] is an elegy for two things – a lost world and a lost love. When the two notes sound together in harmony, it is moving and graceful ..." –*The NY Daily News* "An atmospheric memory play ... with crisp dialogue and clearly drawn characters ... reflects the passing of an era with persuasive insight ... The joy and despair of the musicians is skillfully illustrated." –*Variety* [5M, 3W] ISBN: 0-8222-1721-X

DRAMATISTS PLAY SERVICE, INC.
440 Park Avenue South, New York, NY 10016 212-683-8960 Fax 212-213-1539
postmaster@dramatists.com   www.dramatists.com

NEW PLAYS

★ **CLOSER by Patrick Marber.** Winner of the 1998 Olivier Award for Best Play and the 1999 New York Drama Critics Circle Award for Best Foreign Play. Four lives intertwine over the course of four and a half years in this densely plotted, stinging look at modern love and betrayal. "CLOSER is a sad, savvy, often funny play that casts a steely, unblinking gaze at the world of relationships and lets you come to your own conclusions ... CLOSER does not merely hold your attention; it burrows into you." *–New York Magazine* "A powerful, darkly funny play about the cosmic collision between the sun of love and the comet of desire." *–Newsweek Magazine* [2M, 2W] ISBN: 0-8222-1722-8

★ **THE MOST FABULOUS STORY EVER TOLD by Paul Rudnick.** A stage manager, headset and prompt book at hand, brings the house lights to half, then dark, and cues the creation of the world. Throughout the play, she's in control of everything. In other words, she's either God, or she thinks she is. "Line by line, Mr. Rudnick may be the funniest writer for the stage in the United States today ... One-liners, epigrams, withering put-downs and flashing repartee: These are the candles that Mr. Rudnick lights instead of cursing the darkness ... a testament to the virtues of laughing ... and in laughter, there is something like the memory of Eden." *–The NY Times* "Funny it is ... consistently, rapaciously, deliriously ... easily the funniest play in town." *–Variety* [4M, 5W] ISBN: 0-8222-1720-1

★ **A DOLL'S HOUSE by Henrik Ibsen, adapted by Frank McGuinness.** Winner of the 1997 Tony Award for Best Revival. "New, raw, gut-twisting and gripping. Easily the hottest drama this season." *–USA Today* "Bold, brilliant and alive." *–The Wall Street Journal* "A thunderclap of an evening that takes your breath away." *–Time Magazine* [4M, 4W, 2 boys] ISBN: 0-8222-1636-1

★ **THE HERBAL BED by Peter Whelan.** The play is based on actual events which occurred in Stratford-upon-Avon in the summer of 1613, when William Shakespeare's elder daughter was publicly accused of having a sexual liaison with a married neighbor and family friend. "In his probing new play, THE HERBAL BED ... Peter Whelan muses about a sidelong event in the life of Shakespeare's family and creates a finely textured tapestry of love and lies in the early 17th-century Stratford." *–The NY Times* "It is a first rate drama with interesting moral issues of truth and expediency." *–The NY Post* [5M, 3W] ISBN: 0-8222-1675-2

★ **SNAKEBIT by David Marshall Grant.** A study of modern friendship when put to the test. "... a rather smart and absorbing evening of water-cooler theater, the intimate sort of Off-Broadway experience that has you picking apart the recognizable characters long after the curtain calls." *–The NY Times* "Off-Broadway keeps on presenting us with compelling reasons for going to the theater. The latest is SNAKEBIT, David Marshall Grant's smart new comic drama about being thirtysomething and losing one's way in life." *–The NY Daily News* [3M, 1W] ISBN: 0-8222-1724-4

★ **A QUESTION OF MERCY by David Rabe.** The Obie Award-winning playwright probes the sensitive and controversial issue of doctor-assisted suicide in the age of AIDS in this poignant drama. "There are many devastating ironies in Mr. Rabe's beautifully considered, piercingly clear-eyed work ..." *–The NY Times* "With unsettling candor and disturbing insight, the play arouses pity and understanding of a troubling subject ... Rabe's provocative tale is an affirmation of dignity that rings clear and true." *–Variety* [6M, 1W] ISBN: 0-8222-1643-4

★ **DIMLY PERCEIVED THREATS TO THE SYSTEM by Jon Klein.** Reality and fantasy overlap with hilarious results as this unforgettable family attempts to survive the nineties. "Here's a play whose point about fractured families goes to the heart, mind – and ears." *–The Washington Post* "... an end-of-the-millennium comedy about a family on the verge of a nervous breakdown ... Trenchant and hilarious ..." *–The Baltimore Sun* [2M, 4W] ISBN: 0-8222-1677-9

DRAMATISTS PLAY SERVICE, INC.
440 Park Avenue South, New York, NY 10016 212-683-8960 Fax 212-213-1539
postmaster@dramatists.com www.dramatists.com